Marooned on Australia

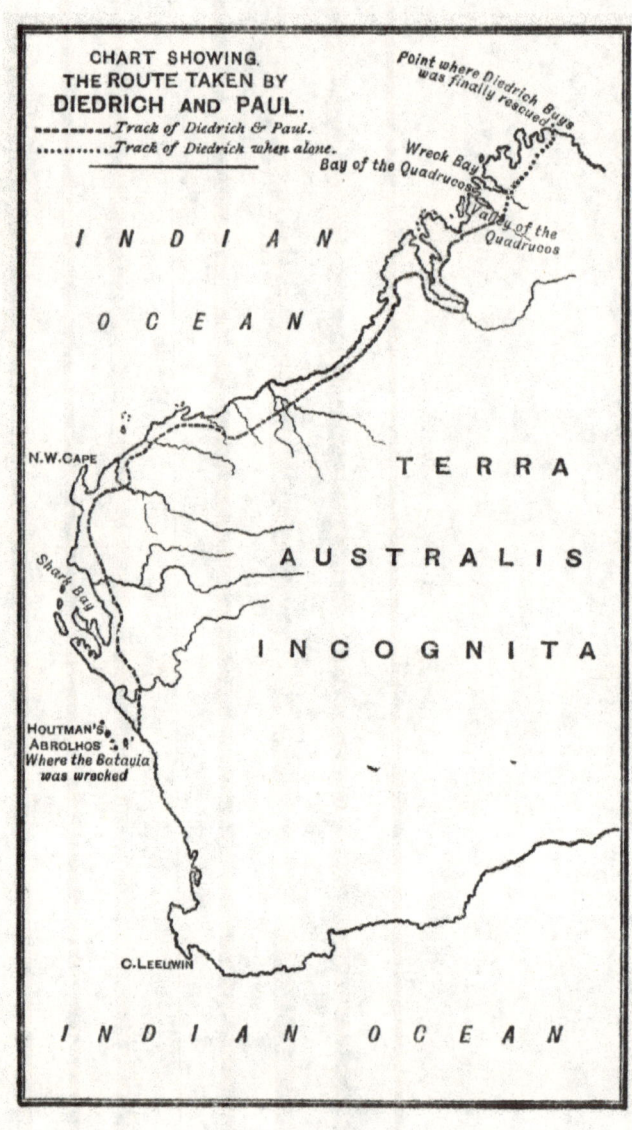

CHART SHOWING.
THE ROUTE TAKEN BY
DIEDRICH AND PAUL.

-------- Track of Diedrich & Paul.
.... Track of Diedrich when alone.
_____ Track of Diedrich

Point where Diedrich Buys
was finally rescued

Wreck Bay
Bay of the Quadrucos

Valley of the
Quadrucos

INDIAN

OCEAN

N.W. CAPE

TERRA

AUSTRALIS

INCOGNITA

Shark Bay

HOUTMAN'S
ABROLHOS
Where the Batavia
was wrecked

C. LEEUWIN

INDIAN   OCEAN

Marooned on Australia

BEING THE NARRATION BY DIEDRICH BUYS OF
HIS DISCOVERIES AND EXPLOITS *IN TERRA
AUSTRALIS INCOGNITA* ABOUT THE YEAR 1630

BY

ERNEST FAVENC

WILDSIDE PRESS

Dedicated to the Memory of my Friend
Edmond Marin de la MESLEE"

by whose accidental death Australia
lost both an ardent geographer and an
enthusiastic student of the history of
the Austral Continent.

                                    ERNEST FAVENC

PREFACE.

IN the following romance I have endeavoured to associate the tradition of De Gonneville's visit to Australia with the historical fact of the wreck of the *Batavia*, and the marooning of two of the mutineers. The wreck of the *Batavia* is perhaps one of the most murderous tragedies that ever happened in any part of the world. One of the ruffians confessed, before being hanged, to having killed and assisted to kill, twenty-five defenceless people. A full account of the wreck and the massacre will be found in *Pinkerton's Early Voyages*.

I have taken a liberty with history in introducing Captain Sharpe, the buccaneer, as in reality he never visited the Australian coast, although some of his crew did. I must also confess to having taken some freedom with chronology as, under the name of Hoogstraaten, I have introduced Abel Janz Tasman many years before his actual advent on the western coast of Australia; and De Witt's voyage of discovery really took place before the wreck of the *Batavia*. I trust, however, that in a romance these inaccuracies will be pardoned.

In the appendix the reader will find an account of the setting up of the great Cross by De Gonneville, and the record of Sir George Grey regarding the head carved on the Rock.

ERNEST FAVENC.

MAROONED ON AUSTRALIA

CHAPTER I

The Wreck of the *Batavia*—The Mutiny—Return of
Pelsart—Marooned.

JEROM CORNELIS! Even now after all the suffering and danger I have gone through, that man's face, the face of the tempter, comes back to me as vividly as ever.

My father was a substantial merchant of Harlem, and in that town I was born, being the second son. That was the age of discovery, and the thirst for it was inherent in nearly every youth. The wonderful success of the Dutch East India Company had fired all men with enthusiasm, and as I grew towards manhood, I longed to make one of the many bands of adventurers who often left for the East. So persistent did I become that my father at last consented to my going, thinking that a voyage would probably cure me. Having some influence with several of the directors of the great company, he obtained for me a subordinate position as clerk to the supercargo on board of the *Batavia*, one of a fleet of eleven ships about to sail from the Texel to Java.

Jerom Cornelis was the supercargo. He had been an apothecary in Harlem, and as such I had known him for some time. He was a man of ability and education, and I had a boyish admiration for him. Now I know him to have been a man whose talents were marred by an intense, almost childish vanity, and a disposition, cruel and relentless as the tiger's. As a lad of eighteen, I saw nothing but the wonderful fascination he exercised, and listened entranced when he dazzled my imagination with pictures of future greatness in the rich islands of the eastern seas.

Our voyage was a stormy one, and as the *Batavia* had over two hundred souls on board, the discomfort was great. I shared a cabin with Cornelis, and in every way that singular man strove to win my affection. Why he did so I cannot say even to this day.

We had been nearly two months at sea, when Cornelis confided to me a plan he had formed, in conjunction with the pilot and some other mutinous spirits, to seize the ship and turn pirate. I endeavoured to dissuade him, but without avail; he bound me over to secrecy and assured me that my life was safe whatever happened, as he would not allow me to take an active part in it, which I certainly had no intention of doing. The plot, however, was frustrated by the weather and other causes, and although I am certain it came to the ears of our commander, Captain Pelsart, he did not, unfortunately, hang the mutineers out of hand as one would have expected from a man of his determination.

Now one would have thought that this would have revealed to me the true character of Cornelis, but such an infatuated fool was I, and so beguiled by his specious tongue, that I still remained his friend and admirer.

We had now doubled the great southern cape, and storm after storm burst upon us with relentless fury. One by one we lost sight of our consorts and at last found ourselves alone; driven out of our course into an unknown sea.

To add to our distress, Captain Pelsart was confined to his berth with sickness and the vessel was in charge of the pilot, who apparently lost all reckoning. It was on the morning of the 4th June, 1629, for the date is indelibly engraven on my memory, that our voyage was brought to a fatal termination by the vessel striking on a reef of rocks. When I got on deck there was nothing visible but white surf and foam everywhere, and we had to wait until daylight, the ship bumping heavily meanwhile.

Daybreak showed us to be in the neighbourhood of a group of rocky islands, one of which was close to us. Finding that the ship was irretrievably damaged Captain Pelsart proceeded to land the passengers and crew on the nearest island. Great confusion ensued and many of the sailors broached some casks of wine in the cargo and got drunk. Provisions were landed, but very little water, and as none could be found on the island, our captain, after two days, started with a boat's crew to the mainland, which we could see in the distance and which was supposed to be the mysterious continent known as Terra Australis.

I had been separated from Cornelis in the turmoil of the wreck, and indeed it was not until the *Batavia* was utterly broken up that he came ashore almost dead. He had been floating for two days on the topmast of the ship, carried backwards and forwards by the current, until at last he drifted near enough to gain the land.

On regaining strength he assumed command, in the absence of the captain, and in spite of all the bloody deeds of that guilty man I will say that he restored some sort of order amongst the demoralized crew and passengers. One of the petty officers named Weberhayes was despatched with some thirty men or more, including some French soldiers in the pay of the Company, to a large island visible to the eastward. If successful in finding water he was to light two fires. The water supply consisting only of rain in the holes in the rock, another smaller party were conveyed to a neighbouring islet.

All this was done in furtherance of a plan maturing in the mind of Cornelis. He retained about him all the ruffians on whom he could rely when the time came to act. This soon arrived. For Pelsart not returning Cornelis threw off the mask. He assembled all his followers at a meeting at which I was forced to attend, and here they all swore a solemn oath to stand by each other, and if Pelsart had gone on to Java and returned with a ship they would endeavour to capture it, if not they would build one out of the remains of the *Batavia*, and start north on a piratical cruise. But first, the mouths of those who could not be trusted had to be silenced for ever.

That night I was awakened by shrieks, groans, and cries for mercy. Cornelis and his myrmidons were butchering in cold blood the helpless people whom they had not admitted to the conspiracy.

I could do nothing during that night of horror, but try and close my ears to the piteous cries of the victims. Nest morning, with their lust for murder still unsated, they went over to the small island and recommenced their fiendish work on the defenceless people. Unfortunately for Cornelis, however, some few escaped and during the night succeeded in making a raft and crossing to the large island, where Weberhayes and his party were. They informed him of the butchery that had taken place and put him on his guard.

The vanity of Cornelis now got the ascendency of him. He had himself proclaimed Governor-general of the barren, rocky islet we were on, which was christened "Batavia's Grave". He had the merchants' chests broken open, and from the stuffs contained therein uniforms were made for a chosen body-guard. This being done, it was determined to exterminate Weberhayes and his men.

Not knowing of the escape of some of the victims, they rowed up confidently, expecting to take the party by surprise, but were surprised themselves. Weberhayes and his followers, armed only with such rude weapons as clubs and stones, fell upon them suddenly, killed some, and forced the others to make a hasty retreat.

Incensed at this repulse, Cornelis led a fresh assault in person and I was ordered into the boat. I had no stomach for the fight, and did not feel particularly sorry when we got more soundly beaten than before.

Weberhayes' party now had arms, taken from the dead mutineers, and Cornelis resorted to treachery. He sent the chaplain, whose life had been spared, to negotiate; and meanwhile he tried to bribe the French soldiers with some of the treasure of the *Batavia*, but they were loyal and at once reported the matter to Weberhayes. A truce was then agreed on. Cornelis was to send over some provisions and receive water in return, of which there was a permanent supply on the island. Weberhayes, however, rightly mistrusted Cornelis and was on his guard; so when a sudden attack was made he was prepared, and not only beat them off with loss, but captured Cornelis.

This was the end of the rebel Governor-general. I never saw Cornelis again until the rope was round his neck.

Now commenced on the island I was on, called "Batavia's Grave", a wild pandemonium. There were still some casks of wine left, and the ruffians drank and quarrelled, and fought with knives over useless pieces of silver. With the capture of Cornelis every semblance of a plan seemed to have vanished. Never shall I forget the horror of that time, although I have seen blood flow like water since. Five wretched women who had been spared from the massacre, two of them being the daughters of the chaplain, were stabbed to death by these devils, and how I escaped a knife through my heart I know not.

At last one morning a sail was in sight, and aided by a fair wind a large ship came swiftly on and soon dropped anchor halfway between the island of Weberhayes and "Batavia's Grave". Hastily arming themselves a large boat's crew from our island started to board the ship. Weberhayes was, however, before them. As Pelsart—for it was he with the *Sardam* frigate—left the ship, intending to land, he was intercepted by Weberhayes who told him the true state of the case. They returned on board and awaited the coming of the other boat. The mutineers, in their gaudy uniforms, were allowed to come well within range. They were then hailed and ordered to drop their weapons overboard and come on board; which they did, and were at once put in irons. Pelsart then landed, but the rest made no resistance and were secured, I being amongst them.

We were kept close prisoners on the island for many days whilst the sailors of the *Sardam* tried to recover the treasure lost in the *Batavia*. Then one day we were taken on board. Some of us were interrogated, some not. I had to confess that I had accompanied one of the armed boats which attacked Weberhayes. There was a short consultation in the cabin, then the deadly work of retribution commenced. One after another the murderers were run up to the yard-arm, and then their bodies were thrown into the sea. Cornelis was hung from a higher yard than the others, in acknowledgment of his leadership. They all died sullenly and defiantly.

As I expected a like death, and had now become used to scenes of bloodshed, I looked on in apathetic despair. At last when it seemed that my turn had come, for there was nobody but myself and a sailor named Paul left, the executions ended; for the ropes were unreeved from the blocks, the anchor raised, some sails set, and the ship stood in for the mainland. Not a word was said to either of us. Paul was an old sailor, and one who had kept his hands as free from bloodshed as possible. He looked inquiringly at me, but I could only do the same to him. Neither of us knew what this meant.

When within a short distance of the land the ship hove to, and a boat was lowered. Our irons were struck off, and we were ordered to get in. A short row took us to a spot where there was easy landing on a beach, sheltered by a rocky reef which broke the surf. When the boat grounded we were ordered out; a couple of bags of biscuit, a breaker of fresh water, a tomahawk, and a cutlass were passed on to the beach. As the sailor who placed these things down stooped near me he whispered something that gave me a clue to our fate. He was one of Pelsart's men and came from my native town of Harlem. The boat's crew shipped their oars and pulled rapidly back to the *Sardam*.

Paul muttered a terrible curse and looked at me. There was no longer any doubt. We were marooned on the coast of the great unknown South Land. To die at the hands of the giant savages said to inhabit it, or the more dreadful strange beasts. What the friendly sailor had whispered to me was, "Keep your heart up. Ships may be round here soon."[A]

So far as I know they never came; when the *Sardam's* masts sank beneath the horizon, both Paul and I had looked our last upon an European sail for many long years.

13

[A]   On his second voyage of discovery Tasman was instructed to call at the Abrolhos, and endeavour to find the two men left by Pelsart; to learn from them all they had found out about the country, and if they desired it, to give them a passage to Java. The record of this second voyage of Tasman's has, however, been either lost or destroyed.

CHAPTER II.

A lonely Night—We make acquaintance with the Natives—Waiting for a Ship—We start for the North—A long hard Journey.

The loneliness of the night that soon closed around us was such as I had never experienced before. Every strange sound or cry of a night-bird startled us from our uneasy sleep on the sand: both of us were heartily glad when daylight banished some of the unknown terrors that had haunted us through the hours of darkness.

After our meagre meal of biscuit and water, I proposed that we should make an excursion a short distance inland, and find out what sort of a place it was where we were abandoned. Paul agreed; and this I must confess here, that, although in after adventures we took opposite sides, and to avenge a great wrong I had to consent to his death, yet during the first years of our miserable exile Paul was the best companion a man could have had.

We hid our water and provisions in a secure place, as we only intended to make a short excursion; then we climbed the low rocks at the back of the beach and found ourselves on a sandy flat, covered with coarse wiry grass. Beyond was a thicket or close forest of low trees and towards this we made our way, Paul armed with the hatchet and I with the cutlass.

We found the thicket barren and grassless, and beyond again was an opening in which we saw, as we thought, a large village of white huts. We listened, but hearing no sound we advanced cautiously towards it. We soon found out our mistake. What we supposed were huts were big mounds of earth built up, as I now know, by a large light-coloured ant. Paul climbed up on the highest of one of these, which was nearly ten feet, and from the top called to me that he could see a low range of hills in the distance, then he came down hastily and whispered that he saw smoke rising a short distance away.

After talking the matter over we agreed that, as we were bound to come in contact with the inhabitants at some time or other, it would be just as well to have it over at once, so we advanced with outward boldness in the direction of the smoke. I confess that my heart sank at the thought of meeting these savage and formidable giants, who were reported to have killed and eaten many of the Company's sailors, but I kept a good face and we were soon close to the place. We came upon them unexpectedly, for they were squatting round two or three fires cooking shell-fish. They raised a great hubbub when they saw us, and most of them ran away, but some raised their lances in a threatening manner.

Both Paul and I gained courage when we saw these Indians, for they were not giants at all, being rather undersized, with thin legs and arms. They were black and quite naked. We shouted to them, and, having read of such things, I broke off a green bough and held it up. This appeared to please them for they lowered their lances, and after some delay allowed us to approach. One of them then gave a peculiar cry, and the rest of the tribe, including the women and children, approached timidly from their hiding-places.

Conversation was of course impossible, but we made them understand at last that we wanted to find out where they obtained their fresh water. They led us to a sandy patch of ground where there was an old tree with white bark. Here a hole had been dug and covered with boughs. On tasting the water it proved to have a somewhat sweet flavour but was quite fit to drink.

Thus relieved of one of our chief causes of anxiety, we determined to make friends with these wretched Indians and, if possible, live with them until another discovery-ship visited the coast; for I believed in the warning whisper of the sailor. I can never understand why my life was spared. Not on account of my youth, for a poor ship's boy, younger than I, was hanged. However, it matters little now.

I pass over the time we spent on this portion of the coast, vainly waiting for the ship that never came. We accustomed ourselves to go without clothes, like the Indians, and they taught us to hunt and what roots and berries were fit to eat. On the other hand our cutlass and tomahawk were very useful, as they had only tools of blunt stone. We kept our clothes carefully, in case of being rescued, but in the course of nearly two years this hope grew faint, and then a bold project entered my head. I began to think that to the north this great Terra Australis must run up very close to Java, and that, if we could make our way there, we might be able to cross by the aid of a raft or canoe to some of the islands and get in the track of the Company's ships. Moreover, the blacks, pointing to the north, had told us that up there lived people who wore clothes. Not like ours, but still they did not go naked. Inquiring still further I found that these people lived on the same land that we were on, the natives being confident that there was no big water to cross. They had never seen these people themselves, as they were a long way off, but they had heard of them from other Indians.

Paul was quite ready to go, when I confided my plan to him, for life amongst these poor Indians was of the most sordid kind, and we could not stand the torment of the swarms of flesh-flies, as could the Indians. They had, however, been very kind to us; for, after all, they could have murdered us at any time and secured the cutlass and hatchet, which they much coveted.

I consulted with Paul how we could reward them, and we finally smashed up the old water-keg, which was now almost useless, and breaking the iron hoops into convenient lengths for knives, distributed them amongst the men of the tribe, who were more delighted with this than if we had given them wallets full of gold.

We had vessels chopped out of soft wood for carrying water, we had learnt how to make fire with two sticks, one old man was coming with us as far as he knew the country, and they gave us a stick with notches cut on it which would ensure our friendly reception by the neighbouring tribe, of whom we had met some members when on our hunting excursions. So we left these poor Indians, who had succoured us in our misery and helplessness, and but for whom we would have died of starvation on that barren coast. They wept and wailed when we turned our faces to the north and left them, for these Indians are like children, easily moved to show emotion, either of anger or grief.

The old man stayed with us three days, then he returned, and we were left alone with an unknown world before us. We journeyed but slowly, for we had to hunt for our food as we went, and that consisted mostly of roots and small vermin, although now and again we managed to secure a large and singular animal which, although possessing four legs, progresses on its hind ones alone, in a series of astounding leaps. It was the time of year when there are many thunder-storms, so that we did not suffer from want of water, and this was of great assistance, for in this dry and hot climate thirst is to be greatly dreaded. We passed through the territory or hunting-grounds of the tribe next to where we had been living without seeing any but a few scattered males, who, as they knew of our existence, did not trouble us or express surprise.

It was a rough journey and we were nearly starved several times. At last we came to a tribe who displayed great hostility at our appearance although none of the others had done so. In fact one tribe had entertained us most hospitably for many months during which it rained incessantly. These Indians, however, would not let us approach them, although it seemed to me that they displayed more fear than anything else.

This made me think that perhaps we were drawing near to the neighbourhood of the strange people who, being evidently more civilized, would in all probability be feared by these other Indians. This I afterwards discovered to be the case.

We found it much harder travelling amongst these hostile or frightened tribes than before, also the days were much hotter and the sun now went right over our heads at noonday so that we had no shadows, which frightened Paul, although usually a bold fellow enough. Moreover, he began to be afraid that we were approaching the country of the giants who had slain the Company's sailors, and I confess that I had my fears of it as well. We fared miserably, as I said before, for not only had we to hunt for a living, but the Indians of these parts are extremely treacherous, and would follow us for miles, seeking an opportunity to drive their lances at us, and another weapon they had, made of bent wood, which made a whirring noise as it flew, and was very hard to avoid. Fortunately, we had now acquired as much practice as these savages, and I warrant they did not come off best in any fair encounters that we had.

Still, it was weary work having to be always on the watch, and dragged us down sorely. At times we followed the sea-shore, when the sandy formation of the coast allowed it, then again we would be forced back into a desolate region of rocks and thickets.

It must have been two years after leaving the place where we were marooned that we came to a hilly, broken region, whereon there were many of the trees that grow straight up for nearly fifteen or twenty feet and then have tops like bunches of grass. The blacks, our first friends, had taught us how to find out the eatable parts of these trees so that we fared better; and, strange to say, in that region we found no inhabitants, nor traces of any. No old camps, no marks of their stone tomahawks on the tree trunks, no traces of man at all. Although this made us wonder it was a great relief to us; and on that account game was plentiful, there being no Indians to keep the animals in check. So we grew stronger and in better heart, travelling slowly and resting often.

The weather was delightfully fine and water plentiful. In this country there is very little difference in the seasons, save that one part of the year is wet and the remainder dry. The rain comes from the north-west, and during the dry months the wind blows from the exactly opposite direction, namely, the south-east.

CHAPTER III.

The Head on the Rock—A strange People—We are made Welcome—King Quibibio.

IT was early one morning that we suddenly came to a Rock on which we both caught sight, at the same time, of a rude carving of a man's head. Much startled, for it was the first sign of human occupation we had seen for some time, we examined it carefully; and we both were struck by observing that this head was not a copy of the natives of the country we had passed through. For these Indians are all most ugly, having blubber lips, flat noses, and low foreheads; but this head was that of a handsome man although without any beard. It was carved in the perpendicular face of the Rock, and the countenance bore a somewhat severe expression; in fact, after such a long and rude separation from any of our kind, both Paul and I felt somewhat awed as we gazed at it.

The Rock bore no other mark nor inscription save this solemn, life-sized head. It was almost on the crest of a rise, and no sooner had we passed it, than we came on to a beaten pathway on which were fresh footmarks, not naked like an Indian's, but more resembling those of a boot without heels.

I confess that this sudden coming upon the fresh traces of a civilized race so unmanned both of us that we felt a strong inclination to beat a hasty retreat. For you must remember that we had now been about four years living either with savages or by ourselves in a wilderness.

"Shall we follow the path?" I whispered to Paul, for I felt afraid to speak loud.

He looked around and then answered in the same low tone:

"Let us look over the ridge."

I nodded assent, and carefully and cautiously we advanced to the top. Hiding behind a heap of rocks we looked over.

What did we see?

The ridge we were on sloped abruptly down the other side, into a beautiful open valley, through which ran a broad river. We saw green patches like cultivated fields, thickets of tall trees, low houses with white walls, and, above all, human beings, clothed and apparently wearing a kind of head-dress. Paul and I gazed speechless with amazement. Then, to my astonishment, he burst out crying and sobbing, and I could not help but follow his example.

When we were somewhat calm, we retraced our footsteps and, having repassed the Rock, halted to debate how we should best approach this strange people. All through our wanderings we had carried with us our jerkins and breeches that we might not appear naked before any civilized race we met. We had, of course, never worn them, and they were still in a fair state of preservation, though weather-stained. Some distance back we had crossed a small runlet; to this we returned and proceeded to make our toilet as best we were able. We washed ourselves carefully, and then did what we could to put our wild hair and beards in order. This was hard work, for the cutlass was too blunt for such work; but by lighting a fire and using the glowing ends of sticks we singed each other's redundant locks down to fair proportions. After we had dressed ourselves, feeling very strange in our unaccustomed clothing, we shook hands with each other and went to meet whatever fate was in store for us.

We had scarcely risen to our feet when we were alarmed by a loud outcry from the very spot on the ridge we had just left. Then followed a strange sound, like the blowing of a horn, and after that all was still.

I said to Paul:

"Let us go on and get it over."

He assented, and we walked up the ridge.

When about half-way up we saw a party of men approaching. They were dressed in a garment like a long shirt, belted round the waist, and wore small turbans. They were all armed and advanced rapidly towards us; one man in front, who wore a shell slung over his shoulder (which was the occasion of the noise we had heard), was pointing to the ground. Evidently it was the discovery of our barefooted tracks that had alarmed them. So intent were they in looking on the ground that it was not until they were comparatively close that they observed us. They stopped short, in silence, although some lifted their weapons.

We made up our minds for instant death, and stood awaiting it, our only weapon being the almost useless cutlass, which I had thrust in the belt of my jerkin. The tomahawk had long since been worn out, and we had thought it better not to carry native weapons.

To our intense astonishment one man suddenly uttered a shout, and all the raised weapons fell. The cry was taken up, and whilst some ran back towards the valley, the others approached with smiles and gestures of welcome. To this, you may be sure, we were nothing loath to respond, and we soon found ourselves being conducted in state towards the valley.

The man who seemed to be in authority spoke volubly in his own tongue, but we could only shake our heads in reply. I noticed that all the party wore sandals of hide, made, as I found out afterwards, from the skin of the jumping animal I have already spoken of.

We were led in a friendly fashion past the Rock with the head carved on it, and then it was that I remarked for the first time that all our escort were beardless, like the head. Both Paul and I, as I may here well state, were fair men, like most of my countrymen, and although our skins were burnt nearly black, our blue eyes and yellow hair showed at once that we were not native Indians.

We were led down into the valley by a broad well-trodden pathway, and on reaching the foot found many people assembling to see us, having been roused by those who ran back. I noticed but few things then, for our excitement was too great, only that the women wore a garment like the men, and the men being all beardless, the only distinction in the appearance of the sexes was that the women wore their hair long, prankt with flowers, parrots' wings, and other adornments.

We soon approached a larger cluster of houses, which I supposed to be the heart of the town, although the town was scattered all up and down the valley. The houses were much the same in design, being but one story high, with flat roofs; but this ugliness was relieved by the sides being made sloping, like the sides of a pyramid. Some of the houses were larger than others by reason of having wings thrown out. They were built of mud and coated with a kind of whitewash to preserve them from the rain. There were flowering shrubs and beautiful trees everywhere, for the valley seemed to be most fertile.

Presently we approached what appeared to be the largest of the houses in the town, if such a scattered lot of houses could be called a town. There seemed to be a good deal of bustle going on, and when we arrived close the crowd parted and a fine-looking man came forward, dressed but little better than the rest, with the exception that his turban was bright red whilst all the others wore white.

He approached us eagerly and looked curiously at us, then said something in a language different from what the others had been using, which sounded somewhat familiar to me, but which I still could not understand. He repeated it, and catching a word that sounded like "ar-me" I said it after him. This delighted him hugely, and he looked at me so kindly that, instinctively, I held out both my hands which he seized and shook warmly, then, leaning forward kissed me on both cheeks. Paul followed my example, and all the people standing around seemed as pleased as possible.

The man with the red turban—whom I may as well say at once was the chief, King Quibibio—led us into the house. For the moment we could scarcely see, the room being darkened to keep out the flesh-flies, which here, as in all parts of Terra Australis, are the greatest possible torment. But as they will not enter a darkened room, the Quadrucos, which is the name of these people, keep their houses darkened. Our eyes soon grew accustomed to the dim light, and we found the interior delightfully cool, on account of the thickness of the walls. There were skins and other kinds of mats about the floor but no seats of any kind, for these people always sit or recline on the ground.

The king motioned us to be seated, setting the example by lying down on a rug. He then called out an order in his own language and a boy came in with two cups made of shells, filled with what I now know to be green cocoa-nut milk. After being so long used to tepid, brackish water I thought it the most delicious beverage I had ever tasted. The boy took back the empty cups and presently came in with a large earthenware bowl of water. He washed our feet, which we submitted to quietly enough, and then proceeded to fasten on each of us a pair of sandals, such as were worn by all the others. This seemed to give the king the liveliest satisfaction, and after motioning the boy to leave he resumed his attempts at conversation.

I may as well here mention that the investiture of the sandals made us members of the family. The meaning of it I will describe later on.

Pointing to himself the king said, "Quibibio", then he pointed to me and I replied, "Diedrich", this, after some repetitions, he succeeded in mastering. Paul was much easier, and then we practised on the king's name until we had it perfectly.

We now had time to look about the room, which was spacious and lofty, and although destitute of any furniture but the rugs and mats, seemed exactly suited to the climate. Doorways opened in two or three directions, and before them hung curtains or screens of reeds. Seeing our curiosity the king led us outside, through the doorway by which we had entered, and taking us a little distance away pointed to the wall. We then saw one reason why they were made sloping. Shallow steps, or rather a stairway, was cut in them to enable the inhabitants to easily reach the flat roof.

Quibibio ascended, and we followed him on to a flat roof surrounded by a low parapet. I never saw a lovelier sight than that beautiful valley presented. The white houses seemed to nestle in clumps of verdure, the cultivated fields, though easily discernible, were not separated by walls, for these people possessed no domestic animals, and they rather regarded the fields as serving as a lure to bring in the big jumping animals from the neighbouring hills. It was a most peaceful scene, and, coming to it suddenly, as we did, out of the great desolate wilderness, we could scarce believe but that we were dreaming.

CHAPTER IV.

A Prince and Princess—The Frenchman's
Cross—Quadruco Customs—Weapons and Drill.

ON descending we found an ample repast laid out on the floor. It consisted of various kinds of game, birds, fish, and boiled herbs. We also found awaiting us two more people, whom Quibibio, by signs, gave us to understand were his son and daughter. I was rather astonished to find these young people so old, as I had taken the king to be only about middle age, but the beardless faces were very deceptive. In fact the only difference noticeable between the Princess Azolta and her brother, Prince Zolca, lay in the length of the hair, and the fact that Azolta wore flowers round her head.

The Quadrucos are a fine race, and as Azolta was a most beautiful girl Paul could not keep his eyes off her during the meal, until I had to tell him that he might give offence. Her twin brother, as I afterwards learned he was, appeared to be of a lively disposition, and to greatly regret that we could not understand each other.

The meal being finished the attendant boy brought round a basin of water for us to wash our hands in; and we then arose from our reclining position, which I and Paul found very irksome.

Azolta retired, as also did Quibibio, leaving his son, Zolca, to entertain us. This he did by smilingly inviting us to walk out. We took our way down a beaten track by the side of the river, which was a broad, sandy stream, with long reaches of water. We soon reached a gorge through which the river descended, or at least the small stream it then was, in a series of cascades. Zolca led us up an easy ascent by the side of this gorge, and we suddenly found ourselves within sight of the ocean. At our feet lay a well-sheltered bay, overlooked by the rise we were on, and beyond was the sea unstudded by a sail. Some large-sized canoes were lying near the beach, and on the rise on which we stood were several men, some with shells slung across their shoulders. Zolca waited quietly until I happened to turn my head slightly, and then I started with surprise, for close to us was reared a wooden Cross, some thirty feet in height.

We approached, and when near it Zolca bent his knee as Roman Catholics do. Paul and I, being of course of the Reformed Religion, did not do so, until it struck me that it would be policy to follow Zolca's example. I whispered this to Paul, and we then both knelt down.

Then we examined the cross. It was firmly put together and well planted in the earth; but the inscription that had been cut on it, of which I could but detect a few letters, had been almost entirely defaced by the weather. The cross was made of a ships' spars, and must have been a prominent object from seaward.

Zolca patted the post that formed the cross, and said, two or three times, a word that sounded like "Gon-vil". This awakened a chord in my memory, which I could not explain until it suddenly flashed before me. And I saw myself a boy in old Harlem, pondering over stories of adventure; and amongst them that of the Norman captain, Paulmier de Gonneville, who discovered a great south land, where he stayed with the natives for six months, finding them very peaceful and gentle, although warlike towards other tribes. My memory now becoming clear, I recalled reading of the great Cross he erected, and how he had taken a prince of the country to France, promising to return with him, which, however, he was prevented from doing.

This, then, was the land, and thus was our friendly reception accounted for. It was more than one hundred years since Paulmier de Gonneville had been there, but the tradition that he would return had evidently been faithfully handed down and preserved. I now saw what course to pursue, and felt thankful that my boyish love of reading about discoveries had given the information.

"Gonneville! Gonneville!" I said eagerly, and the delighted native repeated it. Then he insisted on our returning with him, and on arriving at what may be called the palace, he produced a Latin missal, inside of which I could trace in faded characters:

"*Jean Binot Paulmier de Gonneville. Honfleur, 1503.*"

After deciphering it I read it aloud, much to the pleasure of the two natives, for Quibibio had now joined us. Zolca next produced an old-fashioned, short sword, evidently of French make, but there was no inscription on it. Struck by a sudden thought, I drew the old cutlass I had carried so long and presented it to Zolca, making him understand that it was a present. He seemed

26

at first so pleased with the wretched weapon that he could only look at it with delighted eyes; then he put his hands on my shoulders and kissed me on both cheeks, a French custom handed down, I presume, from Gonneville's time. I heartily wished the performer had been his sister, Azolta, who had entered the room and was gazing shyly at us.

I now, having got a footing, as it were, tried to show them by signs, and drawings on the ground with my finger, what had happened to us; how our ship had been wrecked, how we had lived amongst the Indians—at which both father and son showed signs of disgust,—how we had walked on and on until we came to their country. They seemed to readily comprehend it all, and from that time we were as one of the race, and from the date of giving him the cutlass Zolca was my brother. We at once assumed the Quadruco dress, and every one was our friend.

I will now give some account of these people, it being of course what I have since learned.

They are, or, alas! were, of a light colour, with dark hair and eyes, and as I said before, beardless. They were well built, averaging about five feet eight or nine; extremely good-looking, especially the women, many of the young girls being nearly as beautiful as Azolta. Their dress, which was woven out of the woolly pod of a bush, was a single garment like a long shirt, with a girdle round the waist; it reached a little below the knee, and was the same in both sexes. The men wore a turban, but the women wore only ornamental head-dresses of flowers and feathers. They had little occasion to work, the valley being so fertile, and the hunting was merely a pastime and an exercise. The men had but one wife (Quibibio's was dead), and family affection seemed very strong between them. They had a simple kind of religion, which I don't think was much thought of, and consisted merely in a belief in a Great Spirit, who sometimes was kind, and sometimes angry. They had plenty of dances and games, but very few rites or ceremonies.

The tradition of their origin was that their forefathers, with their wives, came from some far-away island in two large canoes; that they found the valley they lived in almost uninhabited, save for some scattered families of savages who fled at sight of them, and they settled down and had lived there ever since.

Of their wars with the Indians, and with two other nations who came from the sea in big boats, I shall have to speak presently, as I had to take my part in them.

The cocoa-nuts growing in groves up and down the valley of the river were, they told me, brought by their ancestors from the land from which they came. This I could most readily believe, as we had seen none throughout our long journey; nor would the arid country we passed through have supported them. So far as I could make out the Quadrucos, at the time of our visit, numbered 800 souls.

I applied myself diligently to learning the language, and with two such teachers as Zolca and his sister it was easy work. Paul did not make such rapid progress, on account of his want of education, but he could soon make himself understood.

One day Zolca came to me in great glee and showed me the old cutlass, polished up and made as sharp as a razor. Little did I then think to what use I should one day see that keen blade put! I asked him who did it, and he took me to a large house I had never yet entered. In it we found many men at work sharpening and cleaning swords, hatchets, and heavy knives, but all very coarsely and roughly made. I was astonished at the sight, for I had no idea that they had any knowledge of metals, but Zolca informed me that these weapons had been taken from the dead bodies of their enemies, belonging to the two tribes who came from the sea and fought them.

By this time we could fairly understand each other, and Quibibio approached me on a subject which had evidently been troubling him.

"When would I teach them to make swords?"

On inquiry it turned out that de Gonneville when he left promised to return, and told the then king, Arosca, that he would bring back men who would teach them how to make metal, and also how to fight like his people.

I hesitated before replying, and then told the king that I was afraid no metal existed in his land, but that Paul and I would go through the weapons they had, and teach his people how men fought in our country. In saying this I, of course, relied upon Paul, who had once seen military service. This answer satisfied Quibibio, and I held a consultation with Paul, who readily agreed to do something that would raise his importance.

Next day, then, we inspected the weapons they made themselves, putting on one side those captured from the enemy. We found that not only did they all possess serviceable bows and arrows, but, in addition, most of the men were expert slingers, and all could throw the lance with precision. They had, however, no

28

system of fighting, each man acting independently, and this was due to the enemies they had had to deal with.

On first coming to the land, some hundreds of years ago, no doubt, their only foes were the native Indians, whom they called Papoos, and these they easily vanquished. Still, however, they had occasional trouble with them, so a beaten path was marked out around the settlement, and this was traversed twice a day by sentinels. As every Quadruco wore sandals, it was easy to detect a barefooted footmark crossing the path, and it was this which led to our detection. The Indians, however, grew to fear them greatly, which was the cause of the abandoned tract of country Paul and I had passed over.

Then a fresh enemy arose. Men came from the sea in great canoes, half the size of Gonneville's, and nearly as high out of the water. These men were of two races, and although they both attacked the Quadrucos, they also fought between themselves when they met.

Fortunately they had not appeared until the settlement was numerous enough to resist them, and as yet, though some of them had actually landed, none had succeeded in getting beyond the shore. These people used bows and arrows, swords, and another weapon which, by its description, I took to be a blow-pipe. A look-out was constantly kept for these marauders, and the shell which was ingeniously turned into a trumpet was sounded as the signal of danger.

Paul was now made captain, and took the work with pleasure, for I think he felt sore that I had been made so much of, and was anxious to also attract admiration.

With my assistance he divided his men into archers, slingers, and a small body of swordsmen, all of them also being armed with lances. In addition, finding that they had no notion of the use of the shield,—strange to say, for even the Papoos knew about that,—we set some of the artificers to work and soon had some light wooden shields covered with hide, which we taught them how to use, for I had been trained to arms in Harlem, as all youths of my position were.

Time passed quickly and happily. The Quadrucos were delighted with their new employment, and as for me, so long as I could look in Azolta's dark eyes and hear her soft voice, I wanted no more.

CHAPTER V.

The Blowing of the War-Shell—The Fight in the
Bay—Burning a Mongol Junk.

THE season of rains had passed over, and the valley was one mass of verdure and flowers. Azolta, Zolca, and I were wandering along in the early morning when the harsh note of the war-shell came from seaward, and was taken up and repeated again and again. It was a most discordant sound in such a scene of peace, and no wonder that Azolta started and clung to me. Zolca's eyes blazed, and he ran towards the men who were approaching with the tidings. Two large vessels had appeared on the horizon, evidently bearing down towards the settlement.

Thanks to our constant training there was no confusion in gathering our forces. The archers mustered together under Paul; I had charge of the slingers; and Zolca led the small body of men armed with swords and shields. The women had been instructed to prepare plenty of food, and also to have long strips of the stuff of which they made their dresses ready for the wounded. Then we marched to the shore, old Quibibio leading.

The two vessels were still at some considerable distance, so we halted on the top of the rise and watched them approach.

Suddenly I recognized our coming enemies from old engravings in the books of travel, which I had read. They were Mongols. I could tell by their strangely-shaped vessels, with their huge lop-sided sails. I had seen many pictures of these ships and of the people. I turned to an old Quadruco near me and asked:

"Have not these people heads like this"—showing the back of my hand—"and tails on their heads?"

"Yes," he answered.

So I knew then that these were Mongol junks that were approaching, and had not much fear, for I had heard that my countrymen in Java used these Mongol people to work in the fields.

We had erected strong barricades at the foot of the low hills commanding the bay, and along here the slingers and archers were posted in alternate parties. Zolca and his swordsmen lay in readiness to rush down and encounter any who might succeed in reaching the land in spite of our volleys of arrows, spears, and stones.

As there was still ample time, the women went round distributing food and drink to the men, and it was a pretty sight to see with what coolness and cheerfulness they did it. But the fact was that Paul's organization, rude as it was, had infused great confidence in them, after the loose disorderly way they had fought before. Azolta herself brought me some food, and when she looked at me before going away I saw that there were tears in her glorious eyes. Then before I knew what I was doing, I caught her in my arms and kissed her. And this, on the eve of battle, was our first kiss.

The wind now dropped, and the Mongol pirates put out sweeps and came down more rapidly. Evidently some amongst them knew the way, for they came straight into the bay, one leading, and as soon as they got as near the shore as they dared they anchored, lying close alongside each other. All our men kept under cover and maintained a perfect silence, as they had been ordered to do. In this silence we could plainly hear the shouts and orders of the pirates who seemed to be all talking at once. I had small concern as to the result, for I had heard the Company's sailors speak most contemptuously of these Mongols. In this, however, I erred.

Heavy, clumsy boats were now dropped into the water and filled with men, and some of them pulled towards my side of the bay, for Paul and I were now posted on opposite sides. I noticed, however, that only about a third of the boats left the ships, the others remaining as it were in concealment, between the two vessels. This was a simple trick which had however deceived the Quadrucos before and cost many lives. Namely, by a feigned attack they had induced all the Quadrucos to rush to one point, and then sent the remainder of the boats to an unguarded spot. We were prepared for this, and the pirates were destined to receive a lesson.

On they came, three boat-loads, propelling their craft by standing up at the oars and facing the bows. I allowed them to come so close that my men got impatient; but I had my reasons for this, and was delighted to see that all the men at the other side of the bay kept close. When the boats were in quite shallow water I gave the signal, and such a storm of arrows, spears, and stones burst on the astonished Mongols that they turned tail at once. The leading boat had received such a hail of missiles that the men were too staggered to stop her, and with the way she had on, she grounded.

This I had anticipated, and giving the signal agreed on, Zolca and his swordsmen came bounding down, Zolca yards ahead. The Mongols showed but little fight and were cut down and killed without mercy, whilst some of the Quadrucos received but slight wounds. My men kept up a relentless fire on the other two boats as they clumsily turned round, and they must have finally reached their ships half full of dead and dying.

While this was going on Paul told me he had the greatest difficulty in keeping his men close, and had he not succeeded it would have spoilt all. The Mongols, although making a great clamour on board their junks at witnessing the repulse of their party, evidently believed that their stratagem had succeeded, for the remainder of their boats, five in number, now made for what they thought was the unguarded side of the bay. Zolca and his men immediately started round to assist Paul, and I and most of my men followed; which was fortunate, for the leader of this party was more cautious, and ordered his boats to land at different points, so that the attack was at five places at once.

This, however, did not save him or his force, for from their cover Paul's men suddenly assailed them with such a hurricane of arrows, &c., that they dared not approach. This leader, however, kept his boats out of the very shallow water and ordered a number of his men overboard, to land everywhere. The manœuvre caused delay, and by this time Zolca had arrived, closely followed by me and my men, and the pirates struggling in the water, unable to use their weapons properly, were all killed, excepting a few who managed to regain their boats which made back for the junks.

None of our men had been killed and only a few slightly wounded, so well had we taught them to keep under cover, whilst the pirates had lost a boat and over a hundred men killed, besides the wounded. By the capture of the boat we gained a great number of weapons of all kinds, and from the dead bodies many more were taken.

Naturally there was much rejoicing amongst the Quadrucos, and when I met Azolta she kissed me of her own accord.

Meantime the pirates showed no signs of leaving, and, as I now know, these piratical junks were packed full of men.

Paul drew my attention to what they were doing, which appeared to be throwing one another overboard. He explained to

32

me that they were simply killing those who were very badly wounded, and throwing the bodies overboard, this, seemingly, being their barbarous practice.

We next held a conference and came to the conclusion that the Mongols intended to wait until night before attempting another onslaught. After our men had eaten a good meal, and had some relaxation, we formed small camps round the bay, where it would be handy for them to reach their posts when wanted; a close watch being, of course, kept on the pirates.

The bay was now alive with sharks, attracted by the dead, but all the bodies we could get I ordered to be taken to the rocky headlands and thrown into the outer sea. So we soon got rid of the sight of these hideous, yellow, flat-faced monsters, with their bald heads and black tails.

I now called Paul and Zolca on one side and communicated to them an idea which I had conceived. The moon rose about two hours after dark, and it was most likely that the pirates would make their attempt shortly before daylight. I therefore proposed to utilize these two hours of darkness by attacking in our turn. It was now only an hour or so past noon, so that we had ample time to prepare. When I explained my plan Paul grasped it at once, and Zolca, although he did not fully comprehend how it was to be done, would, after the success of the morning, have done anything we desired. I sent for some of the most expert bowmen, and with them we went back to the town, which was rash; but then we could have reached the shore in time had there been any sign of another attack. Paul made these men practise shooting up in the air, so that the arrows would fall straight down as if from a height; he measured off a certain distance, and after a short time they grew very skilful at it, making the arrows drop almost exactly within the mark every time.

Meanwhile Zolca and I started some of the women to make three huge bundles of dry palm-leaves; and these, when finished, were bound together at the top, and a loop attached. We then put them to soak in the palm-oil that we used for our lights at night.

Our preparations were now complete, and we had nothing to do but wait and watch until nightfall. There is but little twilight in this country, and as soon as it became too dusk for the Mongols to see us we sent men to collect all the available canoes. When quite dark Paul and I took the smallest canoe and set out for the pirate junks. Our intention was to cut those boats adrift which had not been taken on board again, but were towing astern. We did not paddle, but I propelled the canoe from the stern by means of a lance, while Paul lay in the prow with one of the sharpest swords we could get, ready in his hand. It was very dark, and once under the tall side of the junk we were comparatively safe.

It was a strange feeling to be so close to these wretches, and hear them jabbering and quarrelling overhead. No order appeared to be kept, for they all seemed talking at the same time and none listening. Cautiously we made our way under the stern, which, sloping outwards, completely sheltered us. Here we noted what we wanted to see for our next move, and then I gently impelled the canoe towards the boats. The tide was rising so that the junks swung shoreward, which was just what we wanted. Four boats were towing astern, and after a few noiseless cuts from the keen blade they were floating towards the land. No alarm had been given, and in a few moments the three boats belonging to the other junk were adrift and following the first four.

We did not wait any longer, but I sculled the canoe straight away at right angles. It was lucky I did so, for a tremendous uproar arose on both ships, somebody having caught sight of the boats drifting away. Thinking that whoever had cut the boats loose must be on board, they directed a shower of arrows after them, taking no heed in our direction. Some of the pirates jumped overboard, but doubtless the sharks took all save one, and he actually swam to one of the boats, and was there transfixed by an arrow from one of his own countrymen, for his dead body lay in the bottom when the boats stranded—which they very soon did, for the tide here rises thirty feet or more and makes very rapidly.

We landed at another part of the beach and began our preparations for the real assault. Zolca was delighted with our safe return, and as our time of darkness was but short, we hurried on with everything.

The hubbub on board the junks still continued, but of that we thought little—they could do no more.

Our picked bowmen were drafted into the boats, and we soon had them stationed at what we calculated was the right distance from the ships. We had judged most admirably, for by the shouts of alarm and fear we could tell that the arrows were falling on the pirates like rain from heaven. Zolca was in charge, and by our instructions he kept up the fire intermittingly, that is to say, he would give them one volley, then, after an uncertain interval, another, so that they did not know when to expect it.

Now our turn came, with the three bundles of oil-soaked palm-leaves and some live coals carefully covered up, we started in the same canoe that had done us such good service already. We pulled to Zolca's boat, and he ordered one vigorous volley which must have made the Mongols skip below again. Then we shot like an arrow, straight as we could paddle, for we had determined to throw off all disguise. The stern of the junk where we had been before was reached in safety, and on the great, creaking rudder we hung one of our fire-bundles, the other two we suspended anywhere we could, driving them fast into their places with three swords we had brought with us for the purpose. Having a lance with us, with a bundle of this same stuff at the head, we floated back a bit, lighted this at the hot coals, and touched off the fire-bundles. All this we were enabled to do unobserved, for the sterns of these junks overhang the water a long way, so that it was like a roof over us; moreover, the pirates were all under cover, expecting another shower of arrows.

The oil-soaked bundles burst into immediate flame. Paul hurled the burning spear on board, where it set fire to the roof of their cooking-house, and we paddled desperately back without any harm. Zolca ordered one more volley, and we drew out of the circle of light and waited.

CHAPTER VI.

The End of the Pirate Junks—Paul discovers

Gold—Azolta and I are betrothed—Death of Quibibio.

I WAS in great hopes that if the junk took fire properly it would communicate the flames to the other one, for these unwieldy vessels are built of most inflammable materials. This was not the case. The other junk's crew cut their cable, and drifted out of reach before the fire got fierce hold; then they put out their sweeps and went out to sea, leaving their companions to their fate. The moon now rose, and we had a full view of the scene. Truth to tell, the spear hurled on board by Paul had done more damage than our fire-bundles. It had ignited the top of the cook-house, and from there it had run up the huge sail and masts, whilst the only damage our fire-bundles had done was to burn the rudder and a hole in the upper part of the stern. This, however, was sufficient to put the junk at our mercy.

The Mongols were apparently working hard to extinguish the fire, but without much avail, for the masts, rigging, and sails were soon all aflame, and presently came tumbling about their ears.

Zolca had all the boats drawn round in a circle to prevent the escape of any of the pirates who might jump over, whilst others on shore watched for the same purpose. I did not see any try it, although the junk burned for some hours, until she seemed to have nothing left to burn. Still she did not sink, and we kept our watch all night. When daylight broke she lay there, black and smoking, but with no signs of life on board. I feel pretty certain that when they saw they were doomed, most of them voluntarily sought death in the flames, for I have since learnt that suicide is a custom of these people. Zolca and some of his men boarded her, and found that she had been burnt clean out, nothing but the hull being left.

Whilst engaged in this we heard a great shouting from the shore, and soon learned that the other junk had run on a reef of rocks just outside the bay, and was now lying on her side with the waves breaking over her. As there is a tremendous surf at this place there was little chance for any of the pirates to have escaped, but to make sure Zolca placed a guard there; but none were ever seen, and the waves soon made short work of the wreck. When the tide was nearly full we towed the burnt vessel as far up the sand as we could, and there broke her up, and got a quantity of iron from her.

Things having come to this happy issue, and all our enemies being destroyed,—that is, for the time, for we did not relax any vigilance in watching for others,—life went on easily and happily, especially for me with my beautiful Azolta.

Soon after our victory over the Mongol pirates Azolta and I were publicly betrothed amidst great rejoicing. Quibibio now seemed to have reached all he had desired. He had been the one to witness the return of men from, as he supposed, De Gonneville's country, who had taught his people how to fight, and now I was betrothed to his daughter, and had promised to live and die in his country. Zolca, too, was untiring in his devotion to me, and would have laid down his life for me.

Paul had set his affections on a very pretty girl, the daughter of one of the principal men, and he was betrothed at the same time. This betrothal, according to the custom of the race, was to last one year, when the marriage ceremony took place.

That year passed peacefully and quietly. Paul and I had a house allotted to us, and wore the red turban; but I now began to notice a change in my fellow-exile. So long as there had been hardships to encounter, and fighting to look forward to, he was one of the best and cheeriest of men, although but a rough sailor without any education. But now the life of ease and indolence seemed to bring all his worst qualities to the front. He had no resources to fall back on, although I tried hard to interest him in the work I was doing, namely, trying to teach the natives new arts and industries. I had succeeded in making a rude kind of paper, and after that the manufacture of ink was easy, and with the pinion feather of a bird for pen I had begun to teach Zolca and others the use of written characters.

Paul took no interest in this. He sighed for the rude joys of his former sailor life, the strong drink, the dancing, the singing, and rough jokes of boon companions. Of dancing and singing we had plenty, but the graceful flower-dances of the Quadruco girls did not suit him when he remembered the clumsy jigs of his sailor days.

One day, when I was trying to rally him, he replied hastily

that he wished he had been hanged at the yard-arm of the *Sardam* frigate before he had come to rot in this place. Then he flung out of the house, and I saw him no more that day.

I was in hopes that when he was married he would become reconciled to our quiet life, where, if we were cut off from the world, we at least were well fed and enjoyed a beautiful climate. But this was not to be. That evening he came to me and proposed that we should build a small vessel out of the timbers of the junk, and make our way north to Java. I reminded him that we should probably be hanged at once as two of the mutineers of the *Batavia*. But he replied that by this time they must have forgotten all about us.

"And if not," he said, sinking his voice, "I have knowledge of what will purchase our pardon readily."

"What do you mean?" I asked.

"There is this valley, and—there is more."

While the tempter thus spoke I saw my old home in Harlem, my parents, who had doubtless mourned me both as dead and guilty, and a longing to return came over me. Then the loving eyes of Azolta, soon to be my wife, blotted out the picture, and I knew my duty.

Since my exile and residence amongst the Quadrucos I had learned to look at things from a far different stand-point than the ignorant boy who sailed from the Texel. Then I saw no harm in the Company occupying the lands of the natives, dispossessing and making slaves of them. I had been taught no better. Now I saw the wickedness of it, and the idea of these peaceful, happy people, who had sheltered us in our distress and treated us with honour and distinction, being handed over to the rapacity of the Company, and the tender mercies of its servants, struck me with horror, and I vowed in my heart that I would fight to the last drop of my blood in their defence, even against my own people.

"What do you mean by more?" I asked Paul.

"There is gold here," he returned. "Plenty of it. I found a lot of stones with veins of the metal, when I was out hunting one day."

He went to the corner where he slept and brought out some white stones in which he showed me yellow streaks which certainly looked like gold.

"I have seen it before," he said, "though not in this shape."

Now this determined me more than ever. Should my countrymen learn of this, nothing would stop them from swarming over the land, and the fate of the Quadrucos would be settled.

"Paul," I said, "have you no gratitude for the people who welcomed us and treated us so well? Do you not know what will happen to them if the Company hears of this place, and establishes a Factory here? Can you say that you have the heart to dream of such a plan?"

"Right well do I know what will happen, Diedrich; but it is a lot that must be theirs sooner or later; you yourself must confess that. Some discovery-ship will poke her nose into that bay some fine morning, and then the thing is done."

"But don't let yours be the hand to do it," I replied.

"I am wearied here," he answered, "and above all, it is so easy to get away; where those clumsy junks go, we can go, and what Master Francis Pelsart did in his boat, from where the *Batavia's* bones lie, we can do easily from here in a better boat, which we will build."

"I would sooner cut off my right hand than consent," I replied. "These people have adopted us, and here I will live and die!"

"For the sake of a pretty savage!" sneered Paul.

Mad with sudden rage at this allusion to Azolta, I drew the short sword I now always wore, and was about to fall on Paul, who drew his and stood upon the defensive.

For a moment we faced each other, then Paul dropped the point of his weapon.

"Let us not quarrel, friend Diedrich," he said; "we have been through too many perils together to try to slit each other's skins now. I will forget this mad scheme of mine, though in truth I am tired of this life."

I knew he was but feigning, but I held out my hand and he shook it, and we returned our weapons to our belts. But from that day there was ill-blood between Paul and me.

I understood it all now. It was not the monotony of the life, for Paul was too rough to mind that; it was the discovery of the gold that had so changed him. Here it was useless to him—no better than common rock; but once free, with the knowledge of its locality, and he could enjoy himself to the end of his days.

Azolta noted my abstraction, but I could not tell her the cause, for I was meditating whether or not I should confide in Zolca. For Paul had not given up his purpose, of that I had felt sure, and although he could do nothing by himself, still he must be watched. The death of Quibibio decided me.

PAUL DREW HIS SHORT SWORD AND STOOD ON THE DEFENSIVE.

The old king died happy. These people did not fear death in the least. All his wishes and hopes had been fulfilled. His son Zolca, who would succeed him in the mildly paternal rule which was all that was demanded from the king of the Quadrucos, was a noble fellow; his daughter was about to be married to me, who was as an adopted son; his enemies by sea had been beaten and destroyed. He was ready to die, and he died calmly, smilingly, with the three of us kneeling beside him.

He was buried beside his ancestors, and Zolca now reigned in his place. The mourning did not last long, for death was looked upon as inevitable; and it in no way delayed my marriage to Azolta.

Paul and I were married on the same day, and I took up my quarters in the palace. Since our outbreak we had been ostensibly on the old terms, but in my heart I knew that Paul had in no way relinquished his purpose.

Zolca now being in supreme command, I resolved to take him into my confidence.

It was a long task, for I had to explain things to him which he had not the experience to grasp. In the first place I had to find out if he knew about the gold; to my astonishment he did, and said he could take me straight there. Of course he did not know about the value of gold, but he had noticed the yellow stuff in the rocks when he had been out hunting. I now explained to him that this yellow stuff was what all white men craved. That some would do anything for it. That if they came to hear of it being here they would come in big ships and take it, driving him and his people out of the valley to wander amongst the Papoos, if they did not do worse. That they would have weapons which his people could not resist. He seemed scarcely to understand me, for in his simple mind all men of my colour were friends, "amis" as the Norman captain had taught his ancestors.

To explain things I asked him what he thought the Mongol pirates would have done had they beaten us instead of our beating them.

"Killed us all," he replied promptly.

"That is what the white men would do, only in another fashion," I told him.

Then, my boyish reading coming back again, I related the story of the Conquest of Mexico and all its horrors.

"Deedrick," he said at last, that being their pronunciation of my name, "brother, why tell me all this?"

Then, though greatly loath, I told him that Paul had found the gold, and that the sight of it had changed his nature. That he had proposed to me to build a vessel and go to where our countrymen lived to the north, and bring them back and show them the gold.

"But why?" he asked, in bewilderment. "Is he not happy here?"

It was cruel work, like kicking a dog who would lick your

41

hand, but I had to do it. I told him that men like Paul had such a desire for gold and all it would buy in our country, that they would do anything to get it; that it made them worse than the pirates; that it turned a good man into a bad man. Be it remembered that crime was almost unknown amongst these people; petty quarrels there were, but nothing more, therefore it was extremely hard for me to explain to Zolca.

I then said that we must not trust Paul; that he was bold and clever, and now that he had set his mind on it he would never let the matter rest.

"But, brother," said the bewildered prince, "why are you not like the others?"

I said that some men had stricter notions than others, and I had had very strict parents; moreover, I loved Azolta more than all the gold in the world.

Poor Zolca! He got up and walked about; then, cast himself on the ground again and I saw great tears in his eyes. It was his first experience of human nature. Of course he had never felt for Paul as he did for me, still he had believed in him. At last he sprung up and his eyes were blazing.

"Deedrick! I will kill him before he shall harm my people!"

Prophetic words!

CHAPTER VII.

Paul attempts Flight—Another Pirate Junk—The Fight between the Junk and the Proa—An ancient Goldmine.

But for the grief and anxiety occasioned me by Paul's conduct I should now have been perfectly happy. With my bride Azolta, and my brother Zolca, and congenial work in the instruction of the people, I could scarcely realize that I was the man, who, as a boy, had been herded with mutineers, and put ashore to starve on the unknown land of Terra Australis.

As for Paul, apparently he had settled down to married life and forgotten his plan of sailing for Java, and bringing the Company's men down to show them the gold and the fertile valley of the Quadrucos; but I felt quite sure that he meant to carry it out on the first opportunity.

My attempt to introduce the use of tables and chairs amongst the Quadrucos was not very successful. Zolca and my wife tried hard to accustom themselves to this new mode of eating and drinking, &c., but I am afraid the others only lay on the floor and looked at the furniture. They took to writing, however, and having concocted a simple code of signs, Zolca and I could communicate easily.

One morning the blowing of the war-shell announced danger from the northern side of the valley. Zolca, Paul, and I, with a body of men whose duty it was to hold themselves in readiness—for we had taught the Quadrucos not to rush on like a rabble, but to do everything according to method—proceeded to the spot. We found that several footprints of the Papoos had been found, crossing and recrossing the beaten path which the sentinels patrolled. As these were not very formidable foes, Zolca and his men proceeded in pursuit of them, and Paul and I returned. Before leaving the place, however, Paul asked me if I had seen the paintings in the caves near where we were. I had heard of them from Zolca, who professed not to know by whom they had been done, but I had never visited the place. Paul led me to it. They were gigantic figures, without mouths, dressed in long robes, with halos around their heads. There were also characters resembling written words on the walls of the cave. I imagined they had been done by the Quadrucos who first landed.

As we went slowly home I noticed that Paul seemed most friendly, he talked about the hardships and dangers we had gone through together, and what a happy life we had suddenly dropped on. In fact I never saw him more subdued and affectionate. Zolca did not return that day, evidently his pursuit had led him further than he expected.

I slept soundly, to be awakened at sunrise by my name being loudly called from outside the house. Hurrying out I found Namoa, one of the principal men of the valley, in a state of great excitement. As day broke, the sentinels on watch for the pirates saw a boat with a white sail leaving the bay. They then missed one of the largest of the boats we had captured from the Mongols.

Paul had started for Java!

I concealed all signs of emotion, and with Namoa made inquiries. We found that Paul had taken with him his wife and her two brothers. How he had wrought upon them to join him I cannot say, but they must have been secretly at work for some time, preparing the sail and mast, &c. This, then, accounted for his plausible manner the night before, to lull my suspicions to rest. Zolca's absence was another chance in his favour, and he seized the opportunity.

I treated the matter lightly, explained that Paul had only gone to try how the boat would sail, as we intended rigging masts on all of them. I surmised that he meant it as a surprise for us, that was the reason he had said nothing about his intended trip.

When Zolca returned, which he did in a few hours, having followed the Papoos for a long distance but failed to overtake them, it was quite a different thing, and his eyes showed me that the untamable savage was still latent in him.

However, I had thought the matter over, and had come to the conclusion that Paul never would reach Java. In the first place, even if he escaped shipwreck, he had a most hazy idea as to its whereabouts; in all probability he would land on some strange island, peopled with savages, and he and his party would be murdered. I considered it would be a miracle if he reached Java, unless he was picked up by one of the Company's discovery-ships. Then again, he could not carry a sufficiency of provisions and water to last him through calm weather, when he could not sail. He had spoken of Captain Pelsart's voyage in the boat, but Pelsart was a navigator with a well-built boat, not a clumsy

Mongol affair; also he had a boat's crew of trained sailors. Altogether I looked upon it as a rash and desperate enterprise that only an ignorant man would undertake, and one sure to bring destruction on the heads of the parties engaged in it.

All this I confided to Zolca, who, I think, understood most of my reasoning and felt reassured. Suddenly our conversation was interrupted by the blowing of the sentinel's shell from seaward. We hastened there and, to our intense surprise, found that the boat with the white sail was returning. Now, although I was glad that this, to a certain extent, confirmed what I had already told Namoa and the rest, still I knew that Paul was not coming back willingly, and this idea was soon made a certainty, for, almost immediately, a Mongol junk came into sight. Paul was evidently running back to escape a worse fate.

I drew Zolca on one side and told him the tale I had told Namoa and urged him to accept it as the best policy. We could settle with Paul privately, meantime we wanted his help to fight the pirates. To this he agreed, and when finally the boat ran up to the beach, I hailed Paul in our own language and told him how to act. He was sharp enough to see the situation, and it was evident that the other Quadrucos had no suspicion of the attempted flight. Paul's companions would, of course, divulge it presently, but not until we had dealt with the junk, and I was anxious to avoid any disunion in our ranks with an enemy in sight.

After our last fight I had carefully gone over the bay and found out the channel leading into it. Also, that this channel passed close to one of the headlands of the bay. On this knowledge my plans had long since been formed in case of another attack. As the junk, which was much larger than either of the former two, drew near, we all took up our stations as before, with the exception that a body of bowmen under Namoa, stationed themselves on the headland commanding the channel.

Apparently these pirates knew the entrance into the bay quite well, and this puzzled me exceedingly, also why they persisted in coming, seeing that they got nothing but hard knocks for their pains. I found out the reason soon afterwards.

The junk came on under a light wind and passed unsuspectingly under the headland, from which suddenly descended on her deck a shower of arrows, spears, and stones. The pirates were helpless, or nearly so, and the wind being, as I said, but light, their progress was slow, and before they got out of range, into the middle of the bay, they must have lost a great many of their crew.

I sent a messenger to Namoa, telling him not to move from his position, for I had great hopes of beating the enemy off before dark, when he could give them a parting salute.

The Mongols now hauled down their sails and prepared to get out their boats. They sent one in to reconnoitre, but so confident was I in our ability to chastise them that I did not trouble to keep our ambush a secret, but, as soon as they were well within range, ordered my men to open fire on them with their arrows, which they did with telling effect, and the boat returned quickly to the junk.

Hardly had they reached the side before the harsh note of the shell was heard from the headland where Namoa was stationed. This was taken up and repeated round the bay. Evidently another vessel was in sight. The Mongols, who were in a better position to look seaward than we were, now began getting their boats on board again, with much shouting and noise. Then they got out long sweeps, and, aided by the wind, which had changed to the south-east, put out to sea, passing under the headland, where Namoa gave them a volley which must have made great havoc.

The other vessel was now in full sight, bearing down rapidly on the junk, which seemed anxious to escape. The new-comer was smaller than the junk, not so high out of the water, and much cleaner built. She was propelled both by sail and oars, and Zolca, who had joined me, told me that she belonged to the nation of brown men of whom his father had told me. I know now that she was a Malay proa. She was evidently bent upon attacking the junk, and the matter being thus taken out of our hands, we all crowded to the two headlands to witness the encounter.

Seeing that they could not get away, the Mongols took in their oars, lowered their sails, and assembled their men on the side the Malays were approaching. When the proa was near enough they discharged such a flight of arrows at her deck that, from where we stood, it looked like a cloud flying from one ship to the other. This reception in no way daunted their assailants, who returned the compliment, and swept up alongside the junk with the intention of boarding. We saw their dark figures, seemingly much more active than the Mongols, leaping on to the deck of the junk and being cut down.

Then the Mongols attempted to board the proa, but were repulsed; and that was the last that we actually saw of the fight, for the wind had freshened, and the two vessels, locked together,

46

were soon carried beyond reach of our sight, that is, so far as the details of the combat were concerned. But they continued side by side until dusk came on. Before that, however, a dense smoke had arisen from one of them, and when it fell dark the watchers on the headland saw a great light for many hours.

Now this was almost the last we saw of any of these pirates, though we had one more visit; but we had worse visitors in store.

The battle being over without any loss on our side—having fortunately had someone else to do the fighting for us—a most disagreeable duty remained. This was the trial of Paul and his accomplices. By my advice Namoa was taken into our confidence, and also another of the head men.

The culprits were brought to the palace, and after due admonition were taken to the great cross of Gonneville, for which the people had a superstitious reverence, and there made to vow that they would never be led to make such an attempt again, under penalty of death for a repetition of the fault. Paul, by my advice, had pleaded that he only wanted to make a trial of the boat, but he was deprived of his red turban and had to wear a white one in future—a punishment for which he did not care the snap of a finger, but which, in the eyes of the Quadrucos, was a great degradation.

If Zolca had had his way he would have made the punishments death, I verily believe, so much had I worked on his feelings by my description of what was to be expected if the East India Company discovered the gold. I persuaded him, however, to make the sentences lenient, in order not to make the offence appear too important.

I now wished to see the place where the gold was, and Zolca and I went there one morning. To my astonishment I saw distinctly, by the signs, that pits had been formerly dug there, and that a large area of land had been disturbed at one time. As the Quadrucos knew nothing of the value of gold it must have been done before their coming to the country. But there was no doubt that it had been the work of some people, for, searching further, I found where one hill had been almost quarried away, and great heaps of broken rocks were to be seen in different places. I remembered the characters in the cave Paul had shown me, and it suddenly occurred to me that they were like the copies I had seen in books of Mongol characters.

Was this an ancient gold-mine, formerly worked by these people, and had the secret of the place been preserved for generations amongst them? Did this, then, account for their persistent endeavours to effect a landing? As I now know that these people are of great antiquity, and religiously preserve their traditions, I believe that I then arrived at the right solution.

CHAPTER VIII.

A Dutch Ship comes in Sight—Paul's Treachery—The Captain lands.

Three years passed peacefully and happily, undisturbed even by the wretched Papoos. Paul seemed to have at last given up his mad notion of endeavouring to reach Java and return to civilization.

One day it struck me to ask Zolca about the carven stone head, and he told me that it was done by a Quadruco in the reign of his grandfather; that this man was very clever at the work, and had done many heads, and also made figures out of mud. Some of these he showed me, and I was much struck with them, also with the thought of this savage genius living and dying unknown amongst his countrymen; whereas, had he been in Europe, he might have been taught to be a great sculptor.

I had now a baby son, but Paul had no children, for which I was sorry, as it might have rendered him quite contented with his lot. For myself I desired no change; if at times I felt home-sick, it was but a passing feeling, and I soon forgot it in the caresses of Azolta and the prattle of our babe.

One day Zolca proposed to me a long excursion to the northward. There was a river there which he had visited as a boy, but which he had never been to since. We went with a small party, well armed, for it was very likely that we would fall in with the Papoos. Paul preferred remaining at home, and as I at last began to trust him, I saw no objection to the trip.

It was three days' journey to the river, which much resembled the one we lived on, only the banks were not so fertile. It ran into a bay similar to ours, except that the entrance was blocked by a reef apparently running right across, for a line of breakers stretched from headland to headland. Game was plentiful in the valley of this river, and we spent a day there hunting.

In the afternoon I was down on one of the headlands, noticing how much the formation of the bay resembled our own, when, happening to look towards the north, I was astonished to see a full-rigged ship in the distance. Hastily calling Zolca I drew his attention to it, explaining that these were the enemies to be feared far more than the pirates. The wind was light, and she was coming on under easy sail, apparently examining the coast-line as closely as she dared. The tide had risen considerably, and the line of breakers had nearly disappeared, so that the entrance to the bay looked smooth and inviting.

I had been extremely puzzled what to do, but had now made up my mind and communicated my idea to Zolca. By my advice we removed all our clothing and made ourselves as like the Papoos as possible; then, retaining all our weapons, we patrolled the headland in full view of the ship. My stratagem succeeded. When opposite the bay she hove to and lowered a boat, evidently with the intention of examining the bay and surrounding country. My instructions were to make a hostile demonstration, but to avoid bloodshed; fire arrows over their heads and around them, but on no account to hit anybody.

The boat came swiftly in, and I noticed the admiration in Zolca's eyes, who had only seen the clumsy rowing of the pirates. Once inside the bay we commenced our mimic warfare. The crew lay on their oars, and the officer in charge stood up and endeavoured by signs to make us understand that he wished to land peacefully. Of this we took no heed, but shot our arrows all around the boat. I could see that the men were getting uneasy, and at last the officer lost patience, and drawing a long-barrelled pistol fired at us. I had warned the others not to show any fear if this should happen; and we only redoubled our gestures of defiance, making as if we would rush into the water, on which crew precipitately backed out. The officer then tried to land in other places, but we followed the boat round until at last he gave it up and returned to the ship. Apparently his report of us and the country was so unfavourable that she hoisted all sail, and, keeping well out from the coast, went on down south before a fair wind, and I had every anticipation that she would pass the mouth of our bay during the dark hours of the night.

My feelings were very strange at thus frightening my countrymen off the coast, when a few years back I would have hailed them with tears of joy; but the change in Paul had so affected me that I could not believe that they would keep faith, even if we allowed them to land and make friends. I was rarely glad, however, that we had succeeded in disgusting them with the country without shedding blood, and still more pleased when, on reaching home, we found that the ship had not been sighted, so that she must have passed in the night.

Still she was a looming danger. She had gone south, and would possibly come back again. Paul said little, and displayed no great interest when he heard of the vessel.

I have said that in this country the seasons were wet and dry, rather than hot and cold. The wet season was now approaching, and squalls from the north-west were frequent. The buildings of the Quadrucos were built on rising ground, they having had some bitter experiences of former floods in the river; but for all that I pointed out to Zolca ancient flood-marks, or what I took to be such, above the site of their present habitation. He only laughed and said that no such flood had occurred as far as their traditions went back.

Strict orders had been issued that, in the event of the strange ship showing from the south, everyone was to remain out of sight. The canoes were removed to a secluded cove, and all marks of occupation effaced from the seaward view. I even proposed taking down Gonneville's Cross, which was a standing invitation for a ship to send in and examine it. Zolca, however, would not hear of it, in fact I am sure the people would not have allowed us to do it. He, however, suggested that we should mask it with boughs in the event of the ship appearing.

My forebodings were too true. Early one morning the glint of a white sail to the southward told us that the discovery-ship was on her way back. The Cross was easily hidden behind some palm-trees which we cut down for the purpose, and we anxiously waited for what would result.

The day was fine, the ship came on at a fair rate of speed, and in about a couple of hours or less was abreast of the bay.

It will be remembered that between our bay and the one to the north there was a great resemblance, and, having formerly passed our bay in the night and not knowing of its existence, I was in great hopes that they would take it to be the one where they had tried to land before, and not think it worth while to examine it again. It would have all happened just as I wished but for the treachery of my old comrade Paul.

Suddenly she changed her course and came close in to the shore. Astonished at this manœuvre I looked round for the cause, which was not far to find. Whilst all eyes had been fixed seaward, the traitor had removed the screen of boughs from the Cross, and, not content with this, had climbed the post and fastened a long streamer of red stuff to the top.

Zolca's eyes were like burning coals, and had the culprit

been in sight it would have fared hard with him. I saw that we must act quickly.

"Order the men back to the town," I said. "Let Namoa see that they all retain their arms and keep in readiness. Also," and I looked Zolca straight in the eyes, "order them to secure Paul, *dead or alive!*"

Our only hope now was to prevent Paul having any communication with the landing-party. The men drew quietly back to the town, and Zolca and I and about a dozen men awaited the coming of the boat which had been lowered and was heading towards us.

We stood grouped on the beach; at our backs, on the crest of the rise, towered the great Cross of De Gonneville, which a second Judas had just contaminated. We must have presented a strange picture to the officers who sat in the stern of the approaching boat.

She ran lightly up the beach and two sailors jumped out and held her, one on each side, while the officers landed. I advanced a few paces to meet them. One was a swaggering, red-faced fellow, with a long, blonde moustache curled at the ends, the very type of men I have seen reeling out of the taverns in Harlem. The other was grave and dignified, and to him I naturally addressed myself.

"May I inquire, sir, your name, and that of your vessel?"

Both men started and stared in amazement, and no wonder, at hearing themselves thus addressed by an inhabitant of Terra Australis.

"Who are you, in the name of wonder?" stammered one at last.

"I am from Holland, and was shipwrecked here many years ago. I have adopted this country as my own, and am now one of these people. This," I said, motioning to Zolca to come forward, "is Prince Zolca, the chief of this country, who bids you welcome."

Zolca, who had been tutored by me, held out his hand and the officer I had been addressing took it respectfully. The fellow with the red face curled his moustache and looked on with a sneer.

"May I inquire the name of your ship?" continued the officer.

Now I knew that this question would be asked and had puzzled much over the answer. I determined to tell the truth, for I had undergone my undeserved punishment.

"My name is Diedrich Buys, of Harlem, I was clerk on board the *Batavia*. Although innocent of any misdeed I was found amongst the mutineers and marooned here by Commander Pelsart."

"Incredible!" said the officer. " 'Tis over a thousand leagues from here to where the *Batavia* struck on the Abrolhos."

"It took us four years to reach here," I said.

"Ah! I heard that two men had been put on shore. Where is your companion?"

"He is here, but absent just now."

"My name," said the officer I had spoken to, "is Hoogstraaten, commander of the *Selwaert*; this is my second officer, Herr Arendsoon."

The gentleman indicated inclined his head haughtily, and I gave him an equally stiff nod.

"Prince Zolca," I said, "wishes me to ask you gentlemen to his house. I will guarantee your safety."

Commander Hoogstraaten bowed an assent; I heard the other whisper something about "a trap", but he was frowned down.

"We first went to the Cross, and I told Hoogstraaten of De Gonneville's visit and how we had been welcomed as friends of his. He had read of the Norman's voyage and was deeply interested in what I told him. We then went forward to the scattered town of the Quadrucos. Hoogstraaten looked with intelligent interest on the strange and novel sights, whilst Arendsoon dawdled along, twirling his moustache and leering at any of the pretty girls we passed; for the Quadrucos, after their usual simple, harmless fashion, had lined the sides of the pathway to see the strangers, although there was no rude pushing or crowding.

Arrived at the palace I invited the two officers in, and Azolta received them as I had instructed her to do. The boy brought cups of green cocoa-nut milk, and Zolca and I pledged our guests. While a meal was being prepared in another room, for we had enlarged the palace, I showed Hoogstraaten the Latin missal and sword left by De Gonneville. Zolca despatched some men to the boat's crew with refreshment.

During our meal I related the details of our journey to the commander, who was anxious to get some knowledge of the country for the Company. I could only assure him that all we had passed through was barren and unprofitable. The natives were half-starved wretches who just managed to live, and that was all.

There was nothing whatever to induce the Company to form set-
tlements. Even the valley we were in was but a small patch of
fertile country surrounded by a wilderness.

Hoogstraaten, who was evidently devoted to his work,
seemed much pleased at obtaining so much reliable information
of the unknown land, and when we rose from our meal, to which
the strangers had done ample justice, he gladly acceded to my
invitation for a stroll up the valley. Arendsoon, who had greatly annoyed me by staring openly and admiringly at Azolta during our repast, excused himself on the ground of being unused
to walking, so he stayed behind.

54

CHAPTER IX.

I fight a Duel—Paul appeals to me to let him go in the Ship—The Secret of the Gold—A Tour of Investigation.

Our stroll up the valley occupied more than an hour, for I had much to say and the commander much to ask of me. Zolca accompanied us, he having whispered to me before leaving that Paul had been found and confined to his house, which was watched by sentries.

As we approached the palace on our return I was astonished by hearing a startled scream. Running forward, what were my feelings to see Arendsoon with his arms round the struggling form of Azolta, attempting to kiss her. In an instant I had torn the fellow away, and dashed him violently on the ground. He sprang up again and drew his sword, but Captain Hoogstraaten stepped between and sternly ordered him to stand. He did not look a pretty picture, for he had gone down in the dust very hard, and one side of his face was white with it. I drew my sword and begged that the matter might be settled there and then.

"You have a right to demand it," said the commander.

"I will not fight with a mutineer and a savage," said Arendsoon, offering to return his weapon to its sheath.

"Nay, sir, but you will!" returned Hoogstraaten in a voice of thunder. "You have grossly outraged this gentleman's" (and he put a stress on the word) "hospitality, and you shall give him satisfaction or go back to Batavia in irons!"

"Come on, then," he said sullenly; but Zolca, calling to me to wait, ran into the house and brought out the French sword, which was more of a match for the hanger worn by my adversary, than the rude weapon I carried.

We had scarcely crossed blades before I knew that I was his master, and I saw by the coward look in his eyes that he knew it as well. I played with him for a bit, and when I had driven him round until his breath came in short gasps and he was evidently at my mercy, I gave him a slight wound in the shoulder, enough to afford him an excuse for leaving off. A great shout of triumph went up from the assembled natives when they saw the blood trickling down his breast.

Captain Hoogstraaten asked me if I were satisfied, and I replied that I was, otherwise, as I had his life in my hands all along, I would have run him through the body. Namoa got some bandages, and the wounded man's shoulder was bound up. A messenger had been despatched for two of the boats' crew. When they appeared, Arendsoon was ready to accompany them, but before he left, the captain demanded his sword, which he unbelted and gave to him.

Hoogstraaten now asked me about the entrance to the bay, and I undertook to show him the channel so that he could bring his ship in and anchor her safely for the night. So favourably had this man's conduct impressed me that I felt greatly moved to take him into my confidence with regard to the gold; but I refrained, and perhaps by doing so some gallant lives were sacrificed.

Zolca and I accompanied the boat in a canoe, and piloted the vessel into the bay. When she was anchored I went on board, Zolca returning on shore to see that an ample supply of fresh provisions, cocoa-nuts, &c., was sent off for the crew.

Meantime I followed the captain into his cabin, where, his curiosity still being insatiable, he questioned me about the history of the Quadrucos, and speculated as to their origin, being evidently a man devoted to such scientific questions.

We were interrupted by the arrival of the canoes with the provisions, and with them came a note from Zolca written in the signs I had taught him. It read:

"Come ashore at once!"

Hastily bidding adieu to the good captain, and telling him that my presence was needed at the town, I went on deck. The sailors were all crowded to the side, looking down with curiosity on the natives who were passing up the provisions. Arendsoon was also on the deck with his arm in a sling. As I passed him he gave a scowl. Then he beckoned to me.

"See here, Herr Mutineer!" he said; "I know the secret of your little valley. Your friend in the bilboes was more communicative than you."

I turned cold at heart, but would not let the villain see it, and passed on with a look of unconcern.

I told Namoa, who was in charge, that, if the captain permitted, the natives could go on board in small parties and examine the vessel, but in case of misunderstanding they must go unarmed. Then I took a canoe and paddled to the beach.

It was true what the scoundrel had said. He had been in communication with Paul. The sentinels were not to be blamed, for their orders were that Paul was not to be allowed to escape. They were too simple to suspect anything. Paul had seen Arendsoon from one of the narrow windows of the house, had called to him, and they had then held a long conversation in their own language. This happened when we were away up the valley. We alone were to blame for affording the opportunity.

I had not had a chance to speak to Azolta before. She told me that after the officer held the conversation with Paul he had commenced to pester her with his attentions trying to express his admiration by looks and gestures. She, in her innocence, did not repulse him as strongly as she should, which gave the ruffian confidence.

It was in no sweet temper that Zolca and I now proceeded to Paul's place of imprisonment. On opening the door I was astonished at the change in the man. The sight of the vessel and the sound of his native tongue had brought back all his worst traits, and obliterated what good had shown on the surface. Instead of the cheery, willing fellow I had known so long there was the ruffling mutineer of the *Batavia*.

"Hullo, bullies!" he cried, in coarse defiant tones. "Come to square accounts with me! Ah! but you'll have to be careful. We are under the guns of a tight ship and they won't let a good citizen of Holland be maltreated by savages!"

This was in our own language, but Zolca guessed the import from the fellow's swaggering air, and his eyes gleamed with rage.

"Silence, you fool!" I replied. "Your friend on board that ship is a swordless coward, at present under arrest. As for you, traitor! ship or no ship, guns or no guns, I'd hang you on one of the arms of that Cross you dishonoured if I saw fit. And you know it!"

Paul's crest fell. "You crow loud, friend Diedrich, but what do you intend? That I signalled the ship 'tis true; but, if you had let me, I would but have gone off as a shipwrecked sailor, and left you and your valley in peace."

"Then," said I, in answer to this palpable lie, "why did you hail that red-faced sot and tell him about the gold?"

"Why? Because I was mad at being bundled in here and locked up like a thief!"

"And locked up like a thief you will be, until the *Selwaert* sails," I replied; "then, as you say, we will square accounts. Are you better than a thief to try to put men on to steal their country from these poor people, who have done you nothing but kindness."

"Diedrich!" cried Paul in an altered tone, "let me go in this ship. I will swear by all I hold sacred, by my mother's grave, that no word of the gold shall pass my lips. Diedrich! I speak the truth. By all the dangers we passed through together, by the many times we have faced death believe me! I am dying slowly here, I must get back to my kind and my country. Do not deny me this chance!"

I was deeply affected by this appeal. Coming from the rude, untutored sailor its eloquence proved its truth. Because I did not feel this great o'ermastering yearning was it not possible for others to feel it?

Paul saw that his words had touched me and coming closer seized my hand.

"Diedrich! once when I was down you stood over me and drove back the Indians who would have killed me. Once when you fell, choking with thirst, I gave you all my share of what water we had, and staggered on until I found some more and brought it back to you. Diedrich! Let your old comrade go!"

"Paul!" I answered, "remember, I am not alone in this. Zolca, whose kindness you have abused, is your judge; it is against him and his people you have sinned."

"But you can persuade him, Diedrich!"

"I will try. Promise me you will remain here quietly and not attempt to communicate with the ship."

"I do, I will!"

I took Zolca's arm and we left the house. I told him what Paul had vowed and promised.

"But," said he, reminding me of what I had clean forgotten, "what is the good of these promises? Is not the mischief done? Did not that fellow whom you fought tell you that Paul had told him all?"

Of course he had. I had remembered this at first, and then, under the sway of memories evoked by Paul's words, forgotten it again. I turned back and re-entered the house.

"Paul, what was the good of those promises," I asked, "when you have already told that officer?"

"I gave him but a hint; I will soon make him believe that I lied to get away from here. If not, rather than that he should

58

bring you harm I will cant him overboard some dark night."

I left Paul in a most undecided frame of mind. When I reached my house I found the evening meal ready, but neither Zolca nor I had much appetite.

"Deedrick," said Azolta suddenly, "why did you not kill that man to-day?"

"Yes, why?" added Zolca. "You could have done it at any time."

I gazed at them for a moment in surprise. Then I remembered their training.

"It was better not," I answered. "We must keep friends with the captain."

I passed a restless night, and early in the morning went down to the beach. The ship swung at her anchor, and I could not help feasting my eyes on her familiar outline, and ceased to wonder at the infatuation of poor Paul. I began to feel something of it myself.

Zolca joined me, and fell to talking about the vessel, and I told him about the sails and their management. Then we took a canoe, and went on board to ask the captain to breakfast. He readily agreed, and after being introduced to the first officer, Herr Vanstrooken, we left for the shore.

During breakfast the captain explained that he was anxious to see the country outside of the valley; not that he doubted my word as to its undesirability, but in his report to the Company he was desirous of saying that he had examined this place himself. We agreed to make the excursion, taking an armed party with us, and men to carry what provisions and baggage we wanted, as we intended to be out one night or more.

We left about ten o'clock, Zolca staying behind in case of any trouble arising. The captain took two sailors with him with firearms, so that we were a strong party. We went by the Rock with the head carved on it, of which Hoogstraaten made a sketch. We then took a sweep round the head of the valley, and camped that night at a small spring.

The secret of the gold having been betrayed to Arendsoon, I had made up my mind to take counsel with the commander of the vessel, although I felt that he would insist upon its being his duty to communicate the information to the Company. However, we were in for it, and must make the best terms we could. It would be better to tell this man voluntarily, than allow him to find it out by accident. It would retain his friendship and assistance.

He was not much surprised, and told me that there had long been a floating rumour of the existence of gold in Terra Australis. He agreed with me that the mines had in all probability been worked by the Mongols in the past.

We then fell to talking of the evil that would accrue to the Quadrucos if the existence of the gold became known, and he, being a man of large experience in the ways of the world, was able to see the matter more clearly than I. He told me that the taking of the country by force and establishing a Factory would only be one of the things to be dreaded. The settlement of the Europeans after a friendly fashion would as inevitably lead to the deterioration and final extinction of the race. The use of liquor—now unknown—would be introduced, and quarrels would arise between the two races.

He told me that much of his life had been spent in the service of the Company, and that in his time he had seen the blighting influence of European contact with the native population. He said he would think the matter over, and see where his duty lay. He would, however, try and put Arendsoon off the scent. Fate, however, took that matter out of our hands.

I slept but badly, for gloomy thoughts of the future were before me, and at daylight I was up.

CHAPTER X.

A Storm—Wreck of the *Selwaert*—Paul relates the events of the Mutiny—Hoogstraaten builds another Vessel.

I WAS struck by the look of the sky when I glanced around. The sun rose red in a haze, looking more like a setting than a rising sun. It was dead calm, and very warm. There had been no dew during the night, and the air was oppressive. Hoogstraaten noticed the same, and with a sailor's instinct, prophesied a storm within forty-eight hours.

Where we camped was on the way to the river which Zolca and I had lately visited, and it struck me that I ought to show the captain the bay, as it might lead him to make a mistake if ever he visited the coast again. I proposed this to him, and he was well pleased at the idea. So we continued north, instead of returning home, having ample provisions with us. I promised the commander that, as we returned, we would go by way of the gold-mine.

The day was oppressively hot, and although no clouds were visible—nothing but a thick haze—a low and constant mutter of thunder seemed to rumble around us. We were all tired when we reached the river, and enjoyed a swim in a large pool which was in the bed just where we came on it.

After eating and resting we went on to the bay in which the river discharged itself.

The captain drew my attention to the clouds now gathering in the north-west; dark and sullen they looked, lit up every now and again by lurid flashes of lightning.

"We are going to have a gale," said Hoogstraaten, "and I am glad that my ship is in safe quarters."

I had heard from the natives that at times terrific winds blew from the north-west, but none of great magnitude had occurred during my residence with them.

As we stood on the beach, gazing at the bay, the captain, to my great surprise, burst into a fit of uncontrollable laughter. Coming from a grave and serious man like my companion, I could scarcely believe my ears.

"Truly, Master Diedrich Buys," he said at length, when he had exhausted his mirth, "I have found you out properly! You and your friends were, I verily believe, the mock Indians who opposed our landing when I examined this bay on our way south."

I now knew the cause of his laughter, and joined heartily in it.

"Were you the officer in the boat?" I asked.

"I was indeed, and your arrows whistled sharply enough about my ears."

It was now my turn to laugh, as I assured him that our fire was harmless; the men being instructed to aim wide.

"I am glad to hear it," he replied, "for I should be loath to think you would have willingly harmed your countrymen, and to tell you the truth I wondered greatly that none of us were hit. I must confess that I fired as straight as I knew how."

Heavy clouds had now gathered over the sky, and a moaning wind had arisen. One of the oldest of the Quadrucos came to me and said:

"We are going to have a great storm, such as I remember once many years ago. We will make places to sleep under behind that ridge, where the wind will not touch us."

This was of course spoken in the Quadruco tongue, and Hoogstraaten looked at me inquiringly.

"He predicts a great storm, and is going to erect shelters for us."

"Ask him about your bay," said the captain.

I guessed at what he meant, and the Quadruco returned answer:

"The waters of the bay are never much troubled, no matter how strong the wind blows."

This relieved the captain's mind.

"Vanstrooken is a good sailor," he said, "and knows well what to do. I can rest easy."

We strolled to the headland and watched the gathering storm. The clouds lying near the horizon to the north-west were of inky blackness, and were cleft every minute by jagged streaks of lightning. The sea looked sullen and angry, and the white crests of waves were already showing.

When we got back we found that the Quadrucos had erected strong comfortable shelters of bark, fresh cut from the trees. That night the wind was something terrible. We lay under the protection of the ridge, but above our heads the storm hurtled, raging amongst the forest trees and rending and tearing the branches. Nothing could stand against its fury.

Towards morning the rain ceased somewhat, and when the dull daylight came, Hoogstraaten and I fought our way to the headland to see the turmoil of the sea. The two sailors accompanied us. The wind and rain had not allowed the sea to rise as high as one would have expected, but the surges that shattered themselves in spray at the foot of the headland seemed to shake it under our feet. Squalls of rain kept sweeping across the ocean, and in the interval between two of these one of the sailors gave a great shout of alarm.

The captain looked up and gripped my arm with a clutch of iron, as a cry of horror burst from his lips. A ship under a rag of storm-sail was driving right on towards us!

A ship! The *Selwaert*!

They were running for shelter and had mistaken the bay. The wind being in my favour I managed to make the Quadrucos hear me, and they soon came hurrying up. The ship was doomed, but we might save some of the crew.

Hoogstraaten was paralysed with astonishment. His ship, which should have been lying snug and safe in our bay, was coming swiftly on to be shattered to splinters at his very feet! By what wizardry had it come to pass?

We could do nothing but wait, and the end soon came. The ship was flung bodily on to the reef, and, as she struck, the masts came down as though they were broken twigs, and a great green wave leaped up and boiled right over her hull. If any cry arose it was lost in the roaring of the storm. When the sea swept past, her deck was clear and empty. Still that great sea saved many lives, for it swept all alike, living and dying mixed with all the lumber of the deck, right over the reef into the sheltered water of the bay. The natives were ready, and plunging in brought all ashore they could see, assisting those who could swim. In all fifteen were saved, amongst them being our prisoner Paul.

The captain gave us no assistance; he still remained like one dazed, standing on the headland watching the seas hammer his ship to pieces.

The worst of the gale had now spent itself, for the clouds began to break and the rain ceased. We marched the rescued men back to the camp as soon as they were recovered sufficiently. I guessed from Paul's presence that there had been a mutiny, and an attempt to run away with the ship. I would not, however, speak to him, but gave orders to the armed natives to guard them closely and kill any who attempted to escape. Then I went back to Hoogstraaten. He had somewhat mastered himself, and taking my arm asked me how it happened. I said I had asked no questions, but it must have been a mutiny, as Paul was amongst them. As we descended, the sea flung a body on to the rocks close to us. We both recognized it. It was Arendsoon!

Arrived at the camp I proceeded to question Paul for the benefit of the captain, otherwise I would not have spoken to him.

"What have you been doing in our absence?" I asked.

"Arendsoon is the culprit; but for him I would have kept my word."

"He is dead," I answered.

"He had a party of discontented seamen on board, and persuaded them to seize the ship during the captain's absence. Zolca was enticed on board, then seized and confined with the others."

"What others?" demanded the captain.

"Herr Vanstrooken, the boatswain, the carpenter, and five sailors."

"Were they on board when you were wrecked, or did you murder them before starting?" I asked.

"Arendsoon would have killed them all, but I would not have it. I saw too much of that when the *Batavia* was wrecked. When we were ready to sail we sent them ashore."

"Did Arendsoon release you?"

"Yes, when Zolca had been decoyed on board, he came ashore with some men and made the natives understand that Zolca had sent him to take me on board."

"When did you sail?"

"Yesterday morning."

"In the face of that storm brewing?" asked the captain.

"Azolta was alarmed at her brother's absence. Had we not gone we should have been attacked, for she was gathering the people together under Namoa."

Brave Azolta!

"We had got well out to sea," went on Paul, "when the storm burst. We rode it out for some time, but at last determined to run back to the bay for shelter."

"And mistook this place for it?"

Paul bowed his head.

"If you have spoken the truth about saving the lives of the

true men," said Hoogstraaten, "you have saved your own. As for you," and he frowned at the half-drowned mutineers. "Friend Diedrich, I think I shall have to trouble you to erect a gallows for me, since I have no longer a ship or a yard-arm to hang them on!"

There were some broken pleadings from the men, but without an answer the captain turned away and in a short time we were on our march home.

We arrived the next evening much to the delight of the people, and their astonishment when they saw our batch of prisoners. Poor Vanstrooken looked very crest-fallen when he met his commander, but it was no fault of his. He and the others had been seized in their bunks and allowed no chance of resistance. As for Zolca he was furious with passion, for, fearing his desperate nature, he had been put in irons during his detention on board.

The storm had flooded the river considerably, but it soon ran down without doing any damage.

Paul's story was confirmed by Vanstrooken. Arendsoon, who appeared to have been a second Cornelis, would certainly have made short work of his prisoners but for Paul. However, he had met his fate, and the fishes were eating him. It was no good detaining Paul a prisoner, in fact he had had little choice, having had nothing to do with originating the conspiracy, so he was restored to freedom.

The other prisoners were tried by their officers, and of course they would brook no interference from me. Hoogstraaten, however, did not hang them out of hand, as he had promised. Their punishment was to depend on their good behaviour between then and the time they reached Batavia.

As soon as the weather became somewhat calm, the captain and his men set to work to build a new boat to depart in. It was tiresome work, for they could only dismantle the wreck at low-tide, but once they got well under way they were able to employ the time of high-tide in the work of construction. As I have said the tide on this coast rises over thirty feet, so there would be ample depth to float over the reef a boat of the size they were building in Wreck Bay, as we had christened it.

In due time the boat was finished, rigged, and sailed down to our bay, to the admiration of the Quadrucos, who felt almost as though they had built it themselves. She was large enough to carry all of the survivors, and in a few weeks the captain anticipated being able to make a start. The end of the stormy season was now nearly at hand, and once the steady breeze from the south-east set in, the voyage to Batavia could be accomplished with little danger.

From Hoogstraaten, who had been on the northern coast of Terra Australis, I learnt the exact position of our settlement, and also that the whole of the great country we were on was as barren on the coast-line as the part we had travelled over. This was the reason that the Company had not established Factories. Where this great land extended to, the commander could not say, for no man had seen the eastern side of it. He had sailed much for the Company, and this was the first time that any mishap had befallen him of any consequence.

He told me about the brown race we had seen attack the Mongol junk; that they were good sailors, and were found all about these waters, and they often came to Batavia in their proas. They were of what is known as the Malaya race, and called themselves "Orang-Laut", or "men of the sea". The Mongols they called "Orang-Kini", and lost no opportunity of attacking and plundering them.

CHAPTER XI.

Disappearance of five of the Mutineers—They come back again—One turns Blacksmith and Armourer—Marriage of Zolca—The Rebellion.

I am now approaching the tragedy which has since often troubled my conscience. Was it justice or murder? I cannot say; then I thought it was justice, but now, looking back, I see that if by chance I misjudged, if I did not sufficiently allow for the pressure of circumstances, and the mad infatuation of the man, it was murder!

It wanted but a week to the captain's departure, when five of the mutineers disappeared. Naturally we thought they had taken to the bush, intending to remain hidden until Hoogstraaten left, not relishing the prospect of risking their necks at Batavia. These five men were the worst and most unruly of the lot, and I by no means wished them to be left behind to corrupt the people with their vices. I therefore helped all I could, in the search we made for them, but without avail. Not a trace could we find, and at last we had to give it up, trusting that the Papoos would account for them.

It was with great regret that we parted with the captain. He told me that, after the benefits and assistance he had received, he would so word his report that we were not likely to be disturbed. He could truthfully affirm that our valley was but an oasis in the midst of a desert. As for the gold, the secret would never be divulged by him. He also promised that, if put in charge of another ship, he would visit us again. We went to the headland and waved him a last farewell as his little craft shot out to sea before the steady trade-wind.

Paul had shown no anxiety to leave; so I began to think that his last narrow escape had sickened him.

We returned to the town, and Zolca and I were discussing our late visitor, when Namoa came with the astounding intelligence that the five missing men were in the town, and, in fact, had never left it. They had been concealed in Paul's house all the time.

When accused of this Paul admitted it, but defended himself

by saying: that he was not going to see countrymen and fel-low-sailors taken away to be hanged; that Hoogstraaten was a man who never forgave, and that these five men were marked men who would assuredly have suffered although the others might escape with lesser punishment.

All this was exceedingly plausible, and there being no reme-dy for it, we had to accept it. I told Paul to bring the men up, and I would speak to them. They assembled, and a truculent-looking crowd they were, although they tried to look their best.

I told them plainly that they did not bring good recommen-dations with them, but as they had thrown themselves on our hands, we would treat them according to their behaviour. I re-minded them that they were entirely at our mercy, and at a word from Zolca or myself, they would be riddled with arrows and lances.

They remained silent for a time, then one of them stepped forward as spokesman.

"We intend to behave ourselves, Captain," he said, "and will obey orders, and work for our food."

This was a blunt, sailor-like speech that pleased me more than a more elaborate one would have done. I told them that some of the natives would help them to build a house, and that I thought they would be of some assistance fishing.

Matters soon resumed their usual course, although we now saw but little of Paul, the sailors proving more congenial compa-ny for him. As I had suggested, they turned their attention to the fishing and seemed contented enough. I was apprehensive that some conspiracy would be hatched, but for a long time I saw no cause to suspect anything. Three of the men were stolid, igno-rant fellows, who could be led for bad or for good by more as-tute minds. Of the other two I had grave suspicions; they were sly and cunning, and would never look a man straight in the eyes. One was a little, active fellow, named Berghen, the oth-er, a great, gross, hulking giant, called Wegelhoe. They were fast friends, and as ruffians, just about equal. As for Paul, I now knew his character well. Swayed by any stronger mind, he was ready to lend the cleverness he undoubtedly possessed, to the first schemer who gained the ascendency over him. I dreaded the influence of these two, and with reason.

Berghen came to me one day and said:

"Captain Diedrich"—which was the title they gave me—"have we your permission to go up north to where the *Sel-*

waert was wrecked, and bring the rest of the wood and iron down here, and anything else we can find that may be useful?"

"Do you propose going by land or sea?" I asked.

"By sea, Herr Captain; with the wind that now blows from morning till night we can sail either north or south."

"You can go," I said, "but Wegelhoe and another man must stay behind as surety, for you know well I cannot yet trust you!"

I saw a sly smile steal over Berghen's face, which he instantly repressed.

"You can keep any two of us you like, Captain. We have promised to obey orders and behave ourselves. Have we not done so?"

"I have no fault to find," I returned; "but for what purpose do you want to recover the wood and iron?"

"There are many things which will be useful in the settlement. I have worked at several trades, and can work in iron."

I believed him so far, but did not credit that it was for the benefit of the settlement they desired to go north. However, it mattered little now. If they intended to try and escape, Batavia was the only port they could make for, and by this time, or long before, Hoogstraaten would have arrived there, and their reception would be anything but friendly. To make matters certain, however, I assured Berghen that, in case of any treachery, the two hostages would straightway be executed.

Wegelhoe, who was of an indolent disposition like many big men, made no objection to remaining as hostage, and the party, led by Paul, departed in two of the largest boats we had taken from the Mongols. By Zolca's permission some of the male relations of Paul accompanied him.

My fears apparently were unfounded. Zolca and I visited the place several times in one of the boats and always found them steadily at work. Berghen was evidently a man who, if he had been possessed of good principles, would have made his way in the world, for he was decidedly a born organizer. They had formed a camp on shore, and worked a certain time each day, and I could see that Zolca was much struck by the order and method that prevailed.

"If we come to a fight, Diedrich," he said, "we must kill that man first."

Instinctively he recognized the master-spirit for evil amongst the men.

In due time nearly all the remains of the wreck were brought down to our bay, and stacked in safety. I had dreaded the discovery of wine or spirits about the vicinity, but Hoogstraaten had taken all provisions away that had been preserved.

Berghen now had a forge erected, having manufactured a rude pair of bellows, and it was pleasant to hear the ring of his hammer, as he turned out rough, but well-tempered swords, knives, &c.

The wet and stormy season came on again and passed. Everybody seemed contented and at peace. The natives never tired of watching Berghen at work, and some of them quickly learnt the rudiments of the art. I had grown more familiar with the man, and lost much of my dislike to him.

"Captain," he said to me one day, "have you looked well for minerals about here? I should say that both copper and iron exist."

I had to confess that I was not skilled in recognizing the ores of these metals, and he then asked to be allowed a party to make search for them. As Paul had, of course, told them of the presence of the gold, it mattered little whether Berghen found the place or not, so I gave my consent, or rather obtained Zolca's, for I left the control of the Quadrucos entirely with him. Berghen was out for many weeks, two or three days at a time, then one day he announced his success. He had found both iron and copper, and showed me the stones he had brought in. One was sheeny and bright, with many colours, another was of a crumbly nature with dark green patches over it, these were samples of copper ore; the third was heavy and dark, and had a metallic ring when struck, this was iron.

Berghen then said that he knew how to construct rude smelting works, with which he could extract the metal from the ore, if I would give him a party of men to assist him, and to carry in a sufficient quantity of ore.

Suddenly a thought struck me, and I asked, if, during his search for the metal, he had come across the gold mine. A moment's hesitation confirmed me in the thought that he had, and meant to keep it secret from me. Then he answered boldly, "Yes," he had.

I asked him what he thought of it, seeing that he had had experience in other countries.

He replied that there was gold there still, no doubt, but that whatever nation had worked the mine formerly had probably taken the best of the gold away. This was my idea, too, and after some further conversation I told him that I would ask Zolca to let him have the men he required.

My suspicions, never quite lulled, had been again roused by the man's hesitation in replying to me about the discovery of the gold; but how was I, with my short experience of the world, and Zolca, with his simple nature, to suspect the hellish plot that was ripening in secret.

Zolca was about to be married, and a great ceremony was to be held in honour of the occasion. The preparations for this, and the building of a new house for Azolta and myself, engaged all our attention.

Zolca was married, with such pomp and show as we could muster, to one of Namoa's daughters—thought by many to be the fairest girl amongst the Quadrucos. All the sailors attended and had places of honour, although I noticed that but for the presence of Berghen, and the mysterious authority that he exercised, some of them would have been rather too free in their manner. It was wonderful how that scoundrel Berghen kept his plans quiet and curbed the tongues of his men. I heard afterwards that he had been in his youth an officer in the army of Saxony, and had been sentenced to execution for treachery, but had managed to escape. All the time he was with me he acted the part of the rough sailor.

It was not until another stormy season had passed that the conspirators threw off the mask and suddenly overwhelmed us with misfortune. Two years had elapsed since Hoogstraaten left, and I was now the father of two children, a little girl with Azolta's eyes having come to us.

The outburst was planned by a master hand. One night I was rudely awakened to find myself in the grasp of the giant Wegelhoe and another of the sailors. I had no time or opportunity for resistance, in an instant I was bound and forced outside. Here I found lights and fires burning, and men hurrying about. To my astonishment I saw that the sailors, including some of the Quadrucos, now wore light breast-plates and back-pieces, also light iron caps, roughly made but quite sufficient to turn the point of an arrow. Berghen was standing at one of the fires, apparently in command. Zolca, Namoa, and others, in a like plight as myself, were there. As I was brought up Berghen addressed me, but without any insolence:

"Sorry to have to put such an indignity on you, Captain, but necessity knows no law. Now will you, like a man of sense and

71

wisdom, appeal to King Zolca to tell his people that if they show fight, it will mean the instant death of you and him and all the rest."

I spoke to Zolca and told him what to do, adding as a bright thought flashed across me:

"Tell them to slip away and hide their weapons."

Berghen now gave one of the men orders to bring up Azolta and Zolca's bride. The man went and presently came back saying that they were not to be found. Berghen turned in fury on Wegelhoe. "You fat knave, did I not tell you that they were to be securely confined in a room and a guard set over them?"

The giant drew his hand across his heavy forehead. "Himmel! Captain" (Berghen had assumed that rank), "did not you tell me expressly that I must not interfere with the women?"

"Bah! I meant here," and he waved his hand over the town. "I gave you strict orders about the ladies," he said, glancing at me, "that they were to be treated with every respect, but to be closely guarded; but your fat brains will not hold two ideas at once!"

Wegelhoe lifted his cap and scratched his head as though to stir his brains up, but he remained silent under the rebuke. Berghen had become the officer once more, and they all felt it. He meditated for an instant; then addressed me again.

"Captain Diedrich, I am about to release one of these men, and send him round with some of my company to collect the bows and arrows from your people. Which one has the most authority?"

I intimated that Namoa was next in authority to King Zolca.

"Tell him that if he attempts to escape the king's life is forfeited."

I told Namoa what he was expected to do, and advised him to tell the people to give up any spare or old weapons they had, in order to avoid suspicion. As Paul was not present, shame keeping him somewhere in the background, I was able to talk freely in the native tongue.

Namoa was released and departed with two of the sailors and some of the disloyal natives. Berghen called after them to stay, he then told me that the Quadrucos could keep their short swords, an act of grace, which, after all, was only an empty condescension; for, as I soon found out, they were armed with long pikes, against which our short swords were vain weapons.

CHAPTER XII.

Azolta's Stratagem—We are Rescued and retake the
Town—The Camp on the Headland—The White Flag.

THE plot to which we had fallen victims had been most cun-
ningly contrived and carried out. Through Paul's rela-
tives—and I have before mentioned that family feeling was
very strong amongst the Quadrucos—a large number of natives
had been seduced into joining the mutineers. There could have
been no feeling of discontent amongst them; it was done by
working on their simplicity and love of change and novelty.
Berghen, too, had excited their admiration by his mechanical
skill.

The manufacture of the breast-plates, caps, pike-heads, and
other weapons had been carried on secretly for nearly the whole
time the forge had been erected. A watch had been kept, and on
my approach these things had always been at once concealed.

The day was breaking as the men returned, bringing the
weapons they had mustered. Fortunately the show was big
enough to prevent suspicion, although Berghen glanced grimly
at some stringless bows and headless arrows.

Berghen, who seemed desirous to keep on good terms with
me, now had us unbound and marched into one of the sailors'
houses. An armed guard was set round, with orders to shoot us
if we attempted to get out. I doubted much if these men would
have shot at their king if he had tried to escape, but the ex-
periment was too dangerous to risk. A weary day passed, but a
woman's wit was working for us, destined to lead to the undoing
of even such a crafty leader as Master Berghen.

In the afternoon Azolta came back alone into the town. I did
not, of course, see what passed, but she had an interview with
Berghen, during which she managed, by means of such broken
scraps of the Dutch language as she had picked up from me, to
make him understand that she had come back to learn the fate of
her husband. Berghen conducted her to our place of confinement
and called me out. His complete success so far had not yet de-
veloped the cruel savagery of the man's nature, and his manner

was easy and even courteous.

I explained to him, after a conversation with my wife, that Azolta, having satisfied herself of my safety, wished to presently return to where she had left our children.

Berghen hesitated, then asked if she would not bring the children back to the house, assuring me that he would have a guard set over it to ensure her against any annoyance.

I thought it better to comply with this request, and Berghen, having instructed the sailor in charge to allow the princess to pass out when she desired, left us and returned to superintend some work he was engaged in. We re-entered the house and Zolca eagerly embraced his sister and asked after his wife.

Azolta now unfolded the plan which had occurred to her to try and carry out, in the event of finding us alive. As she came in she had met many of the faithful Quadrucos who did not care to return to the town at once. These she had instructed to muster at the Rock with the head carved on it, and bring what weapons they had, and as many more men as they could collect without being discovered.

Her next proposal was that Zolca should leave in her place, take command of these men, and by a sudden onslaught rescue us before daylight. I have already mentioned the close resemblance of the twins, which extended to their height, and the plan seemed perfectly easy and feasible.

I did not at once give my consent, for I dreaded, if it should be discovered, that Berghen's vengeance would be sharp and sure. However, at last I was persuaded, and as evening was drawing on, the work of disguising Zolca commenced. Alas! my wife's beautiful hair had to be sacrificed. They had left us our short swords, and with one of these I shore her long locks. These she nimbly interwove in the head-dress she was wearing and put them on Zolca's head. The transformation was complete, and I felt no fear but what it would deceive the guard. Some more touches were added, then Azolta assumed Zolca's turban and belted on his sword. At dusk he issued forth, and took his way unchallenged to the place of meeting. In order to lull all suspicion in the watching sentries, Azolta accompanied him to the doorway and bade him farewell in sight of them.

Our great fear was that Berghen would intercept and speak to the supposed Azolta; but we were fortunate, he was then on his return from the beach where, as I afterwards found out, he had been overlooking the removal of the boats and canoes. In a short time we were able to assure ourselves that Zolca was safe. Later on Berghen came with a sailor, who brought food and lights; but I guessed that his coming was merely an excuse to see that all was right. Azolta, with a sullen look on her face, could not be told from Zolca, and after a few words with me he departed satisfied.

Then commenced a long and weary vigil, for I felt no inclination to sleep. Azolta, who was tired out, slept on one of the mats, and I sat and watched the glow of the fire through the narrow doorway, for there were no doors to the houses, and the duty of our guard was to keep a sleepless watch on the narrow aperture.

During the early part of the night there seemed to be a great stir, but this died down, and about midnight, when the watch was relieved and the great Wegelhoe took charge, all was silent.

As the hours stole on I began to grow anxious. If anything happened, and Zolca did not come, it would be better for us to cut our way out, or die fighting, than wait for morning to discover the exchange of prisoners. My gloomy forebodings were suddenly put to flight. A loud command in Zolca's voice, so close that it startled even me, broke the silence, and a deadly volley of arrows stretched most of the guard low. Then came a rush of feet as with a loud shout they rushed on, my brother's war-cry sounding loud above all.

He had found over a hundred men assembled, and with them had crept up unperceived, close to our place of confinement.

As we issued forth, with Azolta in our midst, the sluggish Wegelhoe, who had been snoring by the fire, reared up his great length, and seizing his pike made at us with it uplifted for a sweeping blow. I jumped on one side, and stabbed him under the arm which, being raised, left part of his body unprotected by back—or breast-plate. He fell like the log he was, and waving my bloody sword, I shouted to Zolca, and Namoa to rally the rest of the people and we would retake the town.

They now poured down to assist us with their concealed weapons, but Berghen, who had at once grasped the position of affairs, was not so foolish as to sacrifice his men against overwhelming odds. Mustering his traitorous natives, he and his sailors formed a rear-guard, and covered their retreat to the shore. Following the example of Paul and myself, they had worn native dress and saved their European clothes. These they had again assumed, and being dressed in leather breeches and high boots, with iron breast-plate, back-plate and cap, they defied our arrows, whilst from behind them their allies poured disastrous volleys into our lightly-clad ranks. Seeing this we contented ourselves with driving them out of the town, meaning to resume the attack with more caution in the daytime.

We returned to collect the dead and wounded. Zolca was for despatching all who wore Berghen's badge, but I begged their lives, representing how they had been led astray by men with stronger minds. Wegelhoe still lived, and on examining his wound I came to the conclusion that the sword-blade had missed any vital part. I hoped he would live, as he would serve as a hostage, to some extent, in the event of any reverse befalling us.

When daylight broke we mustered our men, and found that at least a hundred males, besides women and children, had gone over to the enemy's camp. This included all who were connected with the family Paul's wife came from, either by blood or marriage, and Zolca and I were relieved to find that the disloyalty had not spread beyond.

But where had they gone to? In the retreat of last night, the sailors had not been accompanied by more than twenty men. We were soon to find out. Mustering about two hundred Quadrucos, Zolca and I marched to the beach, leaving the town in charge of Namoa, in case of a sudden attack from an unexpected quarter.

Berghen, we found, had provided against failure as well as success. Knowing how great were the odds against him, in case of any mishap happening he had stocked a camp on the southern headland with provisions, and all the time we had been prisoners, both men and women had been at work throwing up a rampart of earth around this camp, which, being on the headland, could only be approached across a narrow neck of land. All the boats had been secured, and were on an inner beach under cover of the garrison of the camp. Fresh water could be obtained by digging above high-water mark, and fish were plentiful. He was a clever general, was Master Berghen, but I saw him hanged for all that.

We held a council of war to discuss the situation and could only come to one conclusion: that we could not starve them out, and that to carry the place by assault would mean a great loss of men, whilst a repulse would be fatal. That they must be rooted out somehow we all agreed, for with the boats, they could cross the bay at night, land at any unguarded point, and harry us continually.

When we had finished, that is to say, when we had arrived at no conclusion, I strolled over to the forge and smelting place. Here I found a lot of stone broken up, which at once reminded me of the white stone in which I had seen the gold. Secretly, then, they had been obtaining the gold, whilst feigning to be smelting iron. I could not help feeling a good deal of contempt for myself, for being so easily hoodwinked. All the tools, and everything likely to be of any use, had been carried away.

DIEDRICH RALLIES THE QUADRUCOS AND RECAPTURES THE TOWN.

Zolca now called to me that some one in the enemy's camp was trying to attract our attention. On looking, I saw a man standing on the top of the earthwork, waving a white flag.

We marched towards the camp and halted out of bow-shot. I then advanced alone, and the man with the white flag, the meaning of which I had explained to Zolca, met me half-way.

"Well, Captain Diedrich," said Berghen, "you have fairly turned the tables on me, thanks to that drowsy-headed knave, whom you thrust so cleverly under the arm-pit. I bear you no malice, for I love a fair fighter, but why should more blood be spilt? This country is surely large enough for us both to live in."

To this I could only reply that it was not. That during the whole time they had been friendly guests of ours they had been plotting our destruction. How was it possible to trust them?

"I have a fair offer to make," he went on, ignoring my accusation, which, of course, he could not answer. "You do not want or care for the gold. Let us build a vessel, we have ample timber left for it, and after getting as much gold as we can, let us go in peace."

"To return with a crew of ruffians and cannon, and massacre us all!"

"We may return, I admit, but not with that purpose. Did I behave harshly or cruelly when I had it in my power?"

Truth to tell he had not, but he had harboured a purpose in so doing. Before he died Paul confessed to me the whole of the plot. Berghen intended to keep us prisoners for a few days, until, by kind treatment and large promises, he had persuaded more of the natives to join him and disarmed the remainder. His intention then was to repeat the massacre of the *Batavia*, and all of us, men, women, and children, would have been ruthlessly put to the sword.

Of course I knew nothing of this at the time, or I would have held no parley with the ruffian.

"And if I accept your terms will you give up Paul and all your weapons?"

"As for the arms, that is no matter, but as for giving up Paul, that is another question, for I suppose you mean to give him a short shrift!"

"He is the traitor who has brought all this trouble on us! But for him the *Selwaert* would have passed on without knowing of our existence."

"At least he is not responsible for this last attempt, I planned this unaided, and it was only after strong persuasion, and a few threats, that he joined us."

"Those are my terms," I said, "and I will not depart from them."

"We parted at this, and I returned to my party and told Zolca and Namoa—Berghen planted the white flag on the rampart as he climbed over.

What happened in the camp I learnt afterwards. Berghen assembled his men and informed them of the conditions. So far as the sailors were concerned they cared little for Paul, so long as their own necks were safe, and had he not overheard what was said there is no doubt that he would have been privately seized and handed over to us; but he did overhear it, and not liking the prospect he addressed the Indians in their own language, telling them what was proposed, and what his fate would be when King Zolca got him in his power. At once they rose, and Berghen and his men found themselves surrounded by an angry crowd with bows drawn and arrows pointed at them. This put a stop to the negotiations. Berghen had to give in, and mounting the rampart he pulled up the staff with the white flag, made us a mocking bow, and hostilities were resumed.

CHAPTER XIII.

A Night Attack—Appearance of *The Bachelor's* *Delight*—The Pirate Flag—We evacuate the Valley.

THE hostilities were mostly on the side of the beleaguered party. They had erected double ramparts, and well sheltered behind them they defied us with impunity, for they could sweep us off the narrow neck with their volleys of arrows. At night they would cross in their boats and make sudden raids on the outlying parts of the town, forcing us to keep in arms all night. Berghen understood his business. This lasted for a week or more, the moon being against us all the time for a night attack.

At last, when we had about six hours of darkness, we determined to make an effort to oust them. Zolca led the first attack, I followed with a reserve to assist him. We crept up quietly enough, but Berghen was too cunning for us. He had men posted far in advance of the ramparts, lying down on the ground. These gave the alarm, and before we got anywhere near the rampart they were prepared for us. Zolca, however, dashed on with his men, and actually carried the outer rampart and killed a great number of the enemy, although our own loss was heavy. Between the two ramparts, however, the wily Berghen had dug ditches and holes into which our men stumbled and fell in the darkness.

Zolca was forced to retire, and we agreed to renew the attack at daylight at all hazards. No matter what our loss might be we must exterminate them.

The moon rose about the middle of the night, and soon afterwards one of the men on watch drew my attention to a light out at sea. My heart leaped! Could it be Hoogstraaten; if so the camp was at our mercy.

The light was stationary some distance from the shore, and as the fires in Berghen's camp were still alight, they were no doubt waiting for daylight to land, attracted by them.

Daylight came tardily, and revealed a ship lying off the shore; but she certainly was not one of our ships, even I could

80

tell that by her build. When it was quite light there was a movement of men on her decks, and one going aft ran up a flag at her peak. The lazy morning wind freshened for a moment and blew it out. It was black, with something in white in the centre. The black flag! What did I know about it? It was the flag Cornelis had talked of sailing under—it was the pirate flag of murder!

In an instant a shout burst from the enemy's camp, the sailors there were cheering at the sight. Two descended to the beach, and taking one of the boats set off to the vessel.

I hastily explained to Zolca, and those within hearing, that we must retire; that these men in the ship would assist the others; that we must retreat as quickly as we could, for these new men would bring guns and cannons, against which we could not stand. I told Zolca to send half a dozen swift runners ahead to tell the women and men in the town to gather what they could conveniently carry, and make ready for instant departure, for I saw there was no alternative but to abandon the town, for we could not defend it.

Higher up the valley the river ran through a narrow gorge with mountains on either side. This could be easily defended, and at the back we had the range of mountains, from which the river headed, to retreat on. Above this gorge I determined to convey all the people until the ship left. We followed as fast as we could, leaving men posted to watch the pirates and bring us information of their movements.

We found the alarm had spread, and in a very short space of time we were on the march; but none too soon, for messenger after messenger began to arrive with tidings. First that boats were putting off from the ship filled with men. Then that they had landed. At last that they had formed into a band and were marching towards the town.

However, our people were now well on the way, and leaving them in charge of Namoa, Zolca and I, with about a hundred men, remained behind on the ridge commanding the valley, from whence we could safely harass the enemy should they start in pursuit; for we could easily evade them and inflict great damage on all who should attempt to attack us. For I began to entertain hopes that, by constantly annoying them from the fastness of the woods and mountains, I could soon induce them to leave.

The pirates came on slowly and cautiously, evidently expecting an attack. When they found the town deserted they seemingly suspected a trap, for they sent single men ahead to examine the country. We had left Wegelhoe behind, for evidently he was of no value as a hostage, and we had no mind to be bothered with carrying his huge carcass. It was unfortunate for him, because Berghen, as I afterwards learned, on being informed of his presence, went to him, and after abusing him roundly, stabbed the wounded man to the heart.

The pirates did not attempt pursuit when they found that the town was really deserted. We could see them distinctly from our places of concealment, and could distinguish their voices as they called to one another. They were no countrymen of ours, although there were men from many countries amongst them. We waited until nightfall, and then made our way up the valley to our people.

Namoa had selected a good place for a camp, and although we were now outcasts, unjustly driven from our homes, we were grateful that it was no worse, and that we had had time to get our wives and children away in safety, for I remembered to have heard awful tales of the bloodthirsty doings of these men who sailed under the black flag.

The next morning we went down to the gorge and found that we could defend it against any force the pirates were likely to bring against us; for we could safely inflict such loss upon them that they would not be likely to renew the attempt.

They did not try it, however. Finding that they had the town to themselves, they took possession of such houses as they wanted. Unseen by them, we kept watch on their doings. They brought their ship into the bay, and put her on the beach, and cleaned her thoroughly, she being, as I afterwards heard, leaky and very foul with barnacles. But they never gave us a chance to cut any of them off, for they marched to and fro in compact bodies, well armed.

Meantime they played havoc with our valley. What houses they did not occupy they wantonly destroyed. They cut down the cocoa-nut trees to get the fruit. Whatever would burn they burnt.

At the end of a fortnight the ship was again afloat, and anchored in the bay. Now commenced excursions to the goldmine, and heaps of stone began to accumulate on the beach. The wretched Quadrucos who had sided with Paul had to do the carrying of these loads, and dearly they must have repented of their conduct.

At night we heard screams from the women, and one by one they began to straggle into the bush whenever opportunity offered, and we found them wounded, beaten, and dying. When the pirates discovered that they were deserting, they chained them together, and drove them, so chained, backwards and forwards to the mine. But our opportunity had now come, and we hovered around, and not a day passed but what we killed or wounded one of them.

One day we captured one of the crew. He was away from the others, and out of their sight, examining some stones, when Zolca crept behind him and felled him to the ground. While still senseless he was carried away and secured in the camp. When he came to himself we found that he could speak my language slightly, from having served on board one of our ships. He was an Englishman, and when he found that we did not intend to kill or torture him, he became communicative.

The vessel, he said, was English—that is, so far as an outlawed pirate could be said to belong to any nation. Her crew comprised men of all countries, but mostly Englishmen, as were the captain and officers. Her name was *The Bachelor's Delight*, and she had come from the West Indies, round the Cape of Good Hope, there being many armed vessels in chase of her, on account of the piracies committed. The captain's name was Sharpe, and he thought they would not stay much longer, as the gold they found did not answer the expectations held out by Berghen; moreover, they were losing too many men by our never-ceasing attacks, which they could not guard against. In consequence of this there was a coolness between Captain Sharpe and Berghen. He told us about the stabbing of Wegelhoe, and also that the three other sailors had been drunk and useless ever since they had tasted spirits, after such a long period of enforced sobriety: that there were no Hollanders amongst the crew, and therefore they were not made very welcome.

I lay awake all that night, thinking over this information, and by the morning had decided on a course of action.

The Englishman seemed a cheerful, easy-tempered sort of fellow, without much real harm in him, in spite of his presence on the pirate ship, so I made up my mind to trust him. First, I took him to the gorge, and showed him the impregnability of our position. He laughed, and said Captain Sharpe was not such a fool as to expose his men for nothing. What could he gain by attacking us? Pirates fought for booty, not for the love of fighting.

I recognized this reasoning as sound, and now detailed my plan to him. I had my rude writing materials with me, and with the assistance of this sailor, who, strange to say, could both read and write, I composed a letter in English, addressed to Captain Sharpe. I told him that if he delivered up to us the sailors he had found on shore, who had done us great injury, and also allowed the Indians to go free, we would desist from our attacks upon his men, and let him stay and go in peace.

This the Englishman promised to deliver to him without the knowledge of Berghen, and return with the answer. Although I did not think fit to put it in the letter, I gave the messenger to understand that if my request was not complied with I would redouble my attacks on them, even if we sacrificed two men for one. I had no doubt, however, but what my terms would be accepted, for I saw that these men had no honour amongst them, and would at any time sacrifice each other.

I sent an escort with the Englishman to within sight of the town, or rather the ruins of the town.

Zolca's eyes glistened when I told him what I had done. His one burning desire now was vengeance on the men who had destroyed our peaceful life, and laid our homes in ruins.

Next morning the messenger returned. I had placed men to watch for him in case he was attacked by mistake. He brought a written answer from Captain Sharpe, which he read and translated to me.

It was a remarkable letter, and even now the remembrance of it makes me smile. It commenced with some high-flown compliments to myself, Captain Diedrich, and went on to say that he gladly entertained my proposals; that, so far as he was concerned, Captain Berghen and his men were of no interest to him whatever; that but for him he would have held friendly relations with us, cleaned his ship, and departed. As it was, he had lost several valuable members of his crew, and gained a very little gold, nothing like what was represented. He would release the Indians in a few days, meantime he would see that they were not ill-treated. With regard to the others: he would be leaving in about two weeks, and if I desisted from attacking his men, he would have them heavily ironed and left in the town. The letter ended with expressing a hope that he might meet me before his departure.

I noticed that Captain Sharpe passed over the destruction his men had caused to the valley; but then, it was scarcely to be expected that he would refer to it.

I sent back a message that I agreed with his terms, trusting to his honour as a gentleman and a sailor. Also that, if he would trust himself amongst us, the Englishman would guide him to our camp, and I would entertain him to the best of my poor ability. I had a great desire to see this man, who, according to the sailor's account, was as brave as could be, and as firm as a rock, but yet could write letters of empty compliment to a presumed chief of savages, and prided himself on his gentle descent.

The fortnight went by peacefully enough; the captain kept his promise with regard to the Indians, and the poor remnant of them, including Paul's wife, found their way to our camp. They were pardoned, for they had suffered enough, and once more taken back into the tribe. The Englishman arrived one day to say that Captain Sharpe would have much pleasure in accepting my invitation before sailing. I sent back a word of warning, that Paul, Berghen, and the rest, had better be secured at once, else they might get suspicious, and escape to the bush.

We then set ourselves to work to prepare a feast for the pirate captain. Although this part of the valley was not so fertile as the lower part, there were cocoa-nuts growing, and game was abundant. Dishes were prepared in the native manner, for the pleasure of our late enemy.

CHAPTER XIV.

We entertain the Pirate Captain—Return of Hoogstraaten with two Ships—They attack the Pirate—The Mutineers are tried and hanged.

The captain came, guided by the Englishman and accompanied by one of his officers. He was most elaborately dressed, and wore costly lace at his cuffs and neck. He had no arms but a light rapier. The officer was more soberly attired, and was also unarmed, save for a hanger, or short sword. This gentleman, for although pirates, both he and the captain were undoubtedly such, could speak my language fluently, and had evidently come to act as interpreter.

After our first greeting, he assured me from the captain that my advice had been taken, and that Paul, Berghen, and company, were now safe in heavy irons, with a sentry over them. I asked him if their seizure had not surprised them, and he laughed as at a good joke, as he recounted their wonder and amazement.

I presented the captain and his lieutenant to Azolta and King Zolca, and I had to conceal my smiles as I translated, for their benefit, the flowery compliments of the captain. Our conversation was somewhat hampered, as the lieutenant had to translate to me, and I in turn to the others.

We then went amongst the people, and both men seemed much struck with their appearance, and the beauty of the women. Whilst so engaged, our meal was laid, and on our return we sat down to it, and our guests seemed to most heartily enjoy the strange dishes. After it was over, some of the girls entertained us with dances peculiar to the Quadrucos, of which the captain and lieutenant did not seem as though they could have enough.

When the time arrived for the departure of our guests, I had an escort of picked men to accompany them to the outskirts of the town, an attention which seemed greatly to please this singular man.

When we parted he said that his men would march out of the town at daylight, when we would be at liberty to enter it, and resume possession. That he would be busy preparing for sea all the morning, as he intended to leave by the afternoon's tide, but if King Zolca and I would visit him on board at noon, he would be only too happy. Circumstances beyond our control prevented us from fulfilling this engagement.

In the morning Zolca and I, with an advanced guard, marched down the valley to once more take possession of our town. I could see tears in my comrade's eyes as he saw the ruin that had been wrought. The men, too, gazed fiercely around, and I saw that Paul's fate was sealed this time.

We went to look for the prisoners, and found them heavily manacled in one of the houses. Berghen addressed me with a reckless laugh.

"So you have won the game in the long run, Captain Diedrich! Well, it's the fortune of war, and must be accepted."

I could not find words to answer him. I could not revile a helpless prisoner, but the thought of our wrongs made my blood boil. I set trusty sentinels over them, and left without looking at Paul.

About the middle of the morning the women and children began to arrive, and those who still had houses left went to them and made ready to entertain their less fortunate countrymen.

Almost at the same time a messenger came in from the beach with the astounding intelligence that two more ships were outside the bay. We hastened to the rise, and then I noticed that the great Cross of Gonneville had been wantonly cast down. Although not superstitious I did not like to see this, and the natives raised a wail of lamentation.

Outside the bay lay two ships, flying the flag of Holland, and my heart warmed at the sight. On board the pirate ship the English flag was floating instead of the black one formerly displayed. There seemed a good deal of bustle on her decks, and I guessed she was preparing for a fight.

A boat from one of the ships now entered the bay and rowed to Captain Sharpe's ship, and an officer went on board. He remained some short time and then, re-entering the boat, pulled for the beach, and I went down to meet him. What was my delight at recognizing Vanstrooken. We greeted each other warmly, and he inquired of the strange ship, being seemingly somewhat suspicious of her.

Now I had no mind to see Captain Sharpe taken and hanged as a pirate, for although doubtless he richly deserved it, still the man had behaved honourably to me, and I would not betray him.

I therefore replied that she was an English ship, and they had been here some weeks repairing and cleaning the hull of their vessel.

He then asked if I had seen anything of the five mutineers, and I told him of how they had treacherously made us prisoners and taken possession of the town; but that, thanks to the English captain, we had them safe in irons in the town. This proved to be a most unfortunate speech of mine.

He immediately expressed a wish to see them, saying that Hoogstraaten was captain of one of the ships, and had put in here partly to see me and partly to look for them. I could only accompany him back to the town. As we went he gave me an account of their voyage to Batavia and the dangers they experienced.

When we opened the door of the house the culprits gave a start of dismay as they recognized the visitor. It was as though the executioner had looked in at them.

The officer gazed round at them in silence. Suddenly Berghen spoke.

"Herr Vanstrooken, I trust before you hang us that you will blow that cursed pirate out of the water. The wretch who betrayed us."

"What does this mean?" said Vanstrooken, glancing at me somewhat sternly. "Herr Diedrich says she is an English ship."

"English ship she may be," replied Berghen; "but for all that she is the well-known pirate ship, *The Bachelor's Delight*, commanded by the notorious Captain Sharpe."

Vanstrooken gave me a glance of anger which I returned, for my conscience was easy; I had told the truth if not quite all the truth.

Vanstrooken hurried to the shore as fast as he could, and springing into his boat, bade the men give way smartly. As he passed the stern of the pirate he shouted something to which Captain Sharpe took off his hat and made an ironical bow. Immediately after, the English flag was hauled down and the black flag flaunted defiantly in its place. The delay he had gained had enabled him to get his ship clear and ready for action.

As soon as Vanstrooken's boat got alongside, a cannon was fired from the ship, the ball dropping astern of the pirate. No notice was taken of it, the crew being busy getting the anchor up. She was then allowed to drift towards the entrance until the headland sheltered her from the fire of the ships.

Meantime boats full of armed men left the two ships and

came swiftly in to board and capture their prey. They were received with a warm fire; but nothing daunted, they ranged alongside, and the crews commenced to scramble up the bulwarks. They were, however, vigorously repulsed, not one, I think, getting a footing on the deck. Again and again they attempted it, but without success, and at last had to draw off and return discomfited to their ships. There must have been heavy loss on both sides, for I saw the pirates throw many dead bodies overboard.

Evening was now drawing on, and a breeze had sprung up. *The Bachelors Delight* weighed anchor, and, favoured by wind and tide, swept boldly out in the face of her opponents. She had to endure a galling cannon fire as she threaded the channel; but her masts and spars were untouched, and once outside, she unhesitatingly made for her nearest adversary and delivered a broadside into her that must have done great damage. Shooting past she sheered up to the other one and gave her a like compliment; then, with every sail drawing, she went on her course, and the two other ships soon saw that pursuit was hopeless and presently beat back to the mouth of the bay.

Here, the tide being against them, they had to remain until the morning; but a boat was soon coming ashore from one of them. It was dusk when they reached the beach, but I recognized Hoogstraaten. He stepped on land, looking darkly at me, and would not see my proffered hand.

"You keep strange company since my last visit, Master Diedrich Buys!" he said.

"Truly so;" I answered, somewhat nettled. "You left us five well-ordered gentlemen as guests!"

"That is beside the matter," he replied, somewhat haughtily. "Why did you not at once inform Herr Vanstrooken of the true character of that piratical craft?"

"Because the man had kept his word honourably with me, and handed over the men I wanted in irons. Moreover, I think it would have been much to the advantage of all of you if you had accepted my explanation and let him go in peace."

He looked at me for a moment with a black frown, then suddenly laughed.

"Faith, friend, you are right, I believe! That same pirate carried too much metal for us."

He held out both his hands, and our old friendship was at once restored.

"I will be your guest to-night, with your permission," he

said; "but I must send my boat back with a message."

In a few minutes he was ready to go with me to the town, where we were received with great welcome by Zolca and Azolta.

We sat talking until late that night, for he had much to tell and much to listen to. The events of the years since we parted had been stirring with both of us. He had been back to Holland, had visited Harlem and seen my parents—having gone there on purpose to assure them of my innocence with regard to the *Batavia* mutiny. He brought me loving messages from them, and I felt I never could thank him enough for having done, of his own accord, the thing I most desired, namely, my justification to my family.

Next morning early the boats arrived from the ships, bringing off the captain of the other vessel and some of the superior officers. Vanstrooken, I was sorry to hear, had been badly wounded and was confined to his cabin. The ships had entered the bay at daylight and were now anchored where the pirate vessel had lain.

The proceedings were short. The four prisoners, for Paul, of course, was not included in this trial, were adjudged guilty of both mutiny and desertion, either of them punishable with death. They were straightway taken on board and hanged at the yard-arm in their irons. The bodies were then taken out to sea and thrown overboard. They all maintained a sullen silence to the last.

I tried to put off Paul's trial and certain condemnation as long as possible, and in this matter Hoogstraaten unconsciously helped me.

The latter, I may mention, came of a wealthy family, and was a man of considerable private means. He told me that he and my father had joined in bringing me out a few presents, and invited Zolca and me on board to see them.

"I have brought you these," he said, "in case you are again visited by the Malays or Mongols;" and he showed me two brass cannons and a stand of firearms. He told us that he had also a plentiful supply of powder and ball, and moreover, he would leave a sailor with us who was a good gunner, and who would superintend the mounting of the guns in the best position, and also give us instruction in the use of them. This man he would pick up again on his return.

On my asking him of his destination, he smiled slightly.

"To no less a place, Diedrich, than the Abrolhos of Frederic Houtman, where you first made acquaintance with the land of Terra Australis. I am going to try and recover two casks of rix-dollars which went to the bottom when your ship the *Batavia* broke up, and were not recovered by Francis Pelsart. I have on board two native divers from one of the islands of the straits and also one of Pelsart's sailors." I expressed a wish to see this sailor, and Hoogstraaten ordered the boatswain to send him forward.

What was my surprise to recognize the friendly sailor, who had whispered a word of hope to me at the last. He did not know me, however, and it was some time before he could believe that I was the youth he had helped to put ashore so many years ago. I asked him why he had whispered to me of the coming of ships, and he told me that he had overheard Pelsart say—in answer to one of the other officers, whose pity had been touched by our fate—"Rest easy. They will be rescued soon, ships are now under orders to examine this coast."

Hoogstraaten now told me that he had a present for the Princess Azolta, which he must take ashore and give to her himself. It was large and flat, like a board, and the sailors handled it most carefully, the captain himself superintending its transportation. When we reached our house, the sailors behind carefully carrying the mysterious package, I noticed a sly smile on Hoogstraaten's face, as he gravely bowed to Azolta, and requested me to tell her that he had brought her a small present from Europe. The sailors leaned the package against the wall and commenced to strip the coverings off. Hoogstraaten managed to edge Azolta in front of it, as the last covering fell, and she gave a little start and scream of surprise. It was an almost full-length mirror, and she suddenly, and for the first time in her life, saw the reflection of her figure.

The captain's present was an unfailing source of amusement. Zolca had to stand before it and put himself in various fighting attitudes, much to his own admiration. Then his wife came in, and other girls, and the coquetry that went on before that glass was something to remember. Hoogstraaten lay back on a rug, and laughed till he was hoarse.

CHAPTER XV.

The Trial of my Comrade—He wounds Zolca—The Death
of Paul—We destroy the Mongol Junk.

THE captain left for the Abrolhos the next morning, and now a stern duty remained to be undertaken.

Paul had been kept in confinement and closely watched, only his wife being permitted to see him. Namoa had been intrusted with the charge of him, and there was no danger of his escaping, for the Quadrucos had only to look around at their ruined homes and ravaged valley to renew afresh their determination to wreak vengeance on the traitor.

If I could have saved Paul I would. This I solemnly aver, but it was not to be; his deeds had been too black.

I was determined, however, that he should have a trial such as was the custom of civilized nations, and persuaded Zolca that it would make more impression on the people.

Namoa and five other men of standing were then selected, and Paul was warned that the next morning he would be tried for his life.

He asked permission to see me, and, of course, the request was granted. That evening I went to him. He told his wife to leave the house, and we were alone. I sat down by him, and, truth to tell, my heart was heavier than if I had had to face the executioner in the morning. I took my guilty comrade's hand, and we sat for some time in silence.

"I am sorry that they did not capture Captain Sharpe," he said at last.

To this there was no answer to be made, for I thought differently.

"Diedrich," Paul went on, "I did not ask to see you to upbraid you, but you could have saved me if you would."

"How?" I asked.

"When you made terms with Captain Sharpe you could have stipulated that he should take me away and give the others up."

Now, this was another proof of how these men, who were ready to mutiny at any moment, were equally ready to sacrifice their friends to save themselves. Paul cared not a jot for the fate of Berghen and the others, so long as his escape had been provided for.

"Paul," I replied, "when I made terms with Captain Sharpe we were fugitives hiding for our lives. Through your treachery we had to fly to the mountains, and watch our valley and town being destroyed. Is it likely that any thoughts of mercy would find room in my heart just then? Did you attempt to rescue me when Berghen had us confined and guarded?"

Here Paul broke down, and confessed the plot to murder us which I have already detailed.

"I deserve nothing but death, Diedrich," he concluded, "but, at least, I can say that neither when you were surprised, nor during the attack on the camp, did I raise my hand against you or Zolca's people."

This I believed, for I knew well that Paul was brave enough, but yet I had seen nothing of him whilst the skirmishing was going on.

We sat long talking, but I had few words with which to comfort him. I knew his doom was sealed, and he accepted the fact.

I left him towards the middle of the night, and his wife went back to keep him company. He had hinted several times that I should assist him to escape to the bush, but I refused to listen. Not to save Paul's life ten times over would I be guilty of such treachery to Zolca, my brother.

Paul was tried in a large open space in the centre of the town, all the inhabitants being present, grouped round in a circle. I had to preside, as none of the others knew anything about such a mode of procedure. Retribution amongst uncivilized races is short and sharp, without any pretence at trial.

Paul met his coming fate boldly enough. He did not evince any outward fear, although he must have known that death was hanging over his head.

Speaking in the Quadruco language, I appealed to Paul to confess his guilt, and prepare to meet his end; for, if I had had any doubt as to what his fate was to be, one look at Zolca's face would have been sufficient to tell me. The fair valley, now a scene of desolation; the ruined houses; the wreck of what had been a flourishing and fruitful settlement, were there to witness against Paul.

In answer to my appeal Paul acknowledged his misdeeds, and owned that he could no longer be trusted.

I then made an appeal on his behalf, trying to explain, as well as I could in their language, that Paul had been led away by his desire to return to his own people, and that we should keep him a close prisoner until the return of Captain Hoogstraaten from the Abrolhos, who would take him away altogether.

My speech had no effect; I could see that in the faces of all present.

Zolca sprang to his feet and commenced a fiery oration, pointing to all the wreck and desolation around, which excited his audience to frenzy, and I wonder now that they did not rise and slaughter all of those of their own people who had gone over to the pirates. At the conclusion Zolca turned and asked me what to do. In reply I turned to those around, and asked them what punishment they decreed.

"Death!"

The whole crowd shouted the doom, but Paul never blenched, though the word seemed to ring and echo up the valley in a hundred reverberations.

There was silence for a moment.

"What death am I to die, Diedrich?" said Paul, without a tremor in his voice.

I turned to Zolca, and he answered:

"The same death as your friends. Hung up on a rope."

"Never!" cried Paul, and leaping on Zolca he snatched the old cutlass from the king's belt, and, before a hand could be raised, cut him down.

Too late, alas!—for the whole thing was instantaneous,—I caught Paul by the wrists, and even as I did so he was stabbed by every one of the infuriated Indians who could get near enough to do it. I relaxed my grasp and he fell dead, with a dozen fatal wounds in his body.

I next turned my attention to Zolca. The blow had been struck at his head, but in his mad haste Paul had only wounded him on the shoulder, at the base of the neck, and the blood was gushing from the wound. I made the Quadrucos, with the exception of one or two, draw back, and with the aid of strips torn from our dresses, managed at last to staunch the bleeding. A litter was soon made, and on it we carefully conveyed the senseless body to his house.

The dismay of Azolta and Zolca's wife may be imagined, but the former retained her presence of mind, and took her place by her wounded brother. I was almost in despair myself, as I had no knowledge of surgery, and knew that the wound wanted skilful treatment which I could not apply to it, in fact might make matters worse.

In this extremity some one called from outside:

"Captain Diedrich!"

Going out I found the Dutch gunner left behind by Hoogstraaten, who had witnessed the trial from some distance. He asked me about the king, and I told him my trouble.

"That is the reason I came to you," he said. "I have often assisted the surgeon, and when we had that scuffle with the pirate there were a good many cutlass wounds to be attended to. I have some material for dressing in my kit, and if you will allow me I will examine the king's wound."

I could have fallen down and worshipped the man. He went to the house that had been allotted to him, and presently returned with some bandages and a sponge.

When we re-entered the house Zolca had recovered from his faint, which had been caused by loss of blood. His first question was as to the fate of Paul, and he listened with satisfaction to the manner of his death.

The sailor now proceeded to examine the wound, and I told Zolca to lie still without speaking. Although the man's hands were rough and hard, he seemed to understand what he was about. The blood had been soaking through the rough bandages I had applied, but after he had strapped it up in a more skilful manner this stopped, and I felt much relieved.

I then went out to see to the burial of Paul's body, but the sailor told me that the Quadrucos had almost hacked it to pieces, and then taken it to the beach. Going down there I found a number assembled, watching the bay, and learned that they had taken the mangled corpse out and thrown it to the sharks. That was the end of Paul, after escaping death in a hundred shapes.

Now commenced a rather trying time. Zolca's wound healed but slowly, and he himself pined at the inaction of a sick-bed.

Meanwhile there was plenty of work to be done. The gunner proved a blessing indeed, not only did he do the work Hoogstraaten had left him to do, but he attended to the others who had been wounded in the fight, and I ever found him a worthy, honest man.

The Quadrucos soon got their spirits back; the drill at the guns and the work of restoring their houses banished thought from them, and the place soon began to assume something of its old look before war had desolated it.

For me it was different; the sickness of Zolca, and the consequent depression of my wife, affected me greatly, added to which I could not forget the death of my old companion, Paul; for, no matter what his sins had been, we had been comrades together through years of wandering in a desert and unknown land, and I could not forget it.

The gunner had one gun planted on the headland which commanded the entrance, the other on an elevation from whence any ship, escaping the first battery, could be safely bombarded. I think he prayed that a junk might turn up, and, strange to say, his prayer was answered. He was a burly fellow of the name of Hessel, and I am sure that he thoroughly enjoyed his life amongst the Quadrucos, about fifty of whom he had drilled into good musketry-men.

A watch was kept on the headland, day and night, for the return of Hoogstraaten, and one night a light was seen to the northward. This, of course, could not be the discovery-ships, and when the news was brought to me I went and woke Hessel the gunner. He chuckled at the news.

"Wait until daylight, Herr Diedrich, and you will see how I will make the rogues skip!"

He betook himself and his picked men to the battery on the headland, and there awaited the coming of the enemy, and dawn.

Zolca, aroused from his uneasy sleep by the stir and bustle, sent over to me to know what it was about. I went to him and told him. Instantly he insisted on being taken to the beach, so that he might witness the engagement in which he could take no part.

It would have made him worse to deny him, so a litter was soon arranged and we carried him to the great Cross of De Gonneville, now once more erect. Hessel was so confident of his ability to beat off the junk, if it proved to be one, that he had not manned the other battery, therefore I was able to stay by Zolca.

It was a calm, balmy night, not a cloud to obscure the stars, not a sound save the wash of the wavelets on the beach. None could have thought at that hour of all the tragedies that beach had witnessed within the short space of a few years. I sat on the sand by the side of Zolca's litter, and thought of all the trouble our coming seemed to have brought down on these simple, friendly people.

Zolca was not asleep, I felt his unwounded arm move, and

he put his hand on my head, which was leaning against the side of the litter, as he might have done to a child. Some strange sympathy must have told him of what I was thinking, and he put his hand out as if to tell me I was not to blame.

Dawn broke at last, red in the tree-tops behind us, and the quick-growing light soon showed the look-outs on the headland that it was a junk in sight. It was a dead calm, however, and I guessed that Hessel was whistling for a wind to bring the enemy within range.

Soon after sunrise a light wind arose, and the junk, hoisting her great clumsy sail gradually approached the land. So light was the wind, and so slowly did it come, that it was nearly two hours before the junk was close to the entrance. Zolca's excitement was intense and I confess I shared it. I had every faith in Hessel, and knew that he would choose the right moment to open fire, otherwise I would have been by his side.

At last it came, a flash of light, and a roar from the headland, followed by the sputtering volleys of musketry. The junk seemed to reel under it, and a yell and clamour arose from her that appeared to equal the report of the cannon. Hessel now fired again, and this time the clumsy vessel was almost pierced through; her masts fell, and it was evident she was sinking. The wind had freshened and the tide being on the flow, she drifted into the bay. Hessel held his fire for the reason, as he afterwards told me, of not sinking her in the channel.

The Mongols had made no resistance, they were too surprised, nor could they see their enemies. Deeper and deeper sank the doomed craft, and when well within the still waters of the bay she suddenly went down. Then commenced a ruthless massacre; the pirates swimming for their lives were shot, or if they reached the shore, stabbed. I could not have stopped it. The Quadrucos had tasted blood too often, lately, and all the savage in them was aroused.

CHAPTER XVI.

Hoogstraaten again—Zolca recovers—Visit to Wreck
Bay—A Strange Discovery.

NEEDLESS to say, Gunner Hessel was delighted with his success, and undertook to teach the best of his natives the tricks of gunnery, so that no vessel could ever enter the bay. This was good boasting, but could be excused at such a time; moreover, stern Nature finally took it out of all our hands, so far as this matter was concerned.

Zolca had momentarily benefited by the excitement of watching the fight, but I prayed for the return of Hoogstraaten, who had a surgeon on board, for a reaction set in, and the king seemed to grow weaker again.

Meantime the many busy hands had almost restored the town, and, although it would take several years before the co-coa-nut trees grew to their former height and beauty, nearly all other signs of invasion had disappeared; so that when at last the welcome arrival of Hoogstraaten's vessels was announced, he could hardly believe that we could have done so much in such a short time.

He was deeply grieved at the news of Zolca's illness, and how it was caused, and said viciously to me:

"Now, if you had let me hang that fellow with the others this would never have happened!"

The surgeon, too, looked grave, and told me that the king would never recover the use of his left arm. Otherwise, he would probably soon get strong enough to go about.

Hoogstraaten was highly interested in the account of the discomfiture of the junk, and the able manner in which Hessel had handled his guns. He warmly praised him, and the burly fellow grinned all over his face with pleasure, for Hoogstraaten was a man both loved and feared by his crew. He was the man of that age and those seas, and I trust that his name as a navigator and discoverer will live for ever.

In return he told me that they had been successful in their search for the two casks of rix-dollars, and that he had been able to map out the coast more accurately than his predecessors had done.

Under the care of the surgeon, Zolca grew better, and was able to walk about with his useless arm in a sling. Hoogstraaten had delayed his departure as long as he possibly could, in order that Zolca might have the attendance of the surgeon. He now had to leave, and it was with the deepest regret I parted from him. Vanstrooken had recovered, and the little cloud between us had passed away.

Zolca, Azolta, and I stood on the beach after bidding Hoogstraaten farewell, and watched his boat speed swiftly to his ship. Once he stood up in the stern and waved his hat to us, then he went on board, the boat was hoisted up, and with a favouring wind the two discovery-ships threaded the entrance to the bay and so stood out to sea.

As they passed the headland Namoa and some of the trained men stationed there fired the gun, in compliment to Hessel. The ships dipped their flags and each fired a gun in reply; then they spread all canvas for the north, and that was the last my companions ever saw of the gallant and generous Captain Hoogstraaten. I saw him again, but under far different circumstances.

The next few months were busy ones. Zolca fretted over the uselessness of his arm; but his health was soon restored, and that made him more contented with his lot.

Things began to smile once more in the valley; the girls danced and sang as before in the calm, soft evenings, and wore flowers in their hair, and the old peaceful life seemed to have come back again.

As I had never been along the coast to the north I proposed to Zolca to take the largest boat we had, and with a few men sail up to the bay where I first saw Hoogstraaten, or "Wreck Bay" as we had named it. Zolca was tired of inactivity and gladly consented.

We started, taking some of our men with their firelocks, and a good supply of provisions. Azolta could not accompany us on account of the children.

Leaving the bay we found the shore to the north fringed with mangroves, so that we could not see dry land. Creeks and openings were common amongst these trees, and up some of them we went; but they led to nowhere, and we always had to return. Dismal-looking places these creeks were. Nothing could be seen on either hand but mud and ooze and the stems of these strange trees which grow in a distorted manner from many roots, and when the tide is low these roots are left bare.

Here I saw for the first time the crocodile, such as I had seen in pictures of Egypt. It was like a huge lizard, and it lay on a little patch of sand, basking in the sun. Neither Zolca nor the Indians had ever seen this gigantic reptile before, and they did not seem to like to approach it; for these creatures never came in to our bay, being, for aught I know, frightened of the sharks. I whispered to the men to fire at it, and with one accord they fired a volley at it. This roused the brute effectually, although it did not seem to be badly wounded, or scarcely more than tickled. It lashed out its tail and plunged into the water. When the men saw its great length and girth and enormous jaws, they made sure it was coming to attack the boat and, taking to the oars, pulled away with a will. I, too, thought it would have been better to have let the brute alone; but it did not come near us, and we saw no more of it.

However, we did not enter any more of these dismal creeks, and coming on to a nice open beach without any surf, we landed and rested for the night. About the middle of the following day we reached Wreck Bay.

All signs of the unfortunate *Selwaert* had disappeared; but the camp on the shore where the men had been working still remained. Here we camped for the night and slept soundly enough, all save Zolca who was always restless now. In the middle of the night he roused me up and drew my attention to a light on the other side of the bay.

"Papoos!" he whispered.

I did not think so, for I knew from my experience that the Papoos made many fires when they camped. Here there was but one. I persuaded Zolca to wait until daylight, for he proposed to steal round and fire a volley into the camp in the darkness. By my advice he agreed to wait until it was light enough to find out the cause of the fire.

When morning came we went round and found that the Papoos had been there and set fire to a dry log, which had been smouldering for some days; the wind during the night had freshened it into a flame. But this was not all, the Papoos had been there in large numbers and a fight had taken place. A fight and more than a fight; a feast as well—for these black Indians are cannibals and eat one another.

Zolca and the other Quadrucos looked at the remnants of human bodies in deep disgust, for the Quadrucos were very dainty eaters; they preferred the flesh of fish and fowls and, above all, the vegetables that they grew and the green cocoa-nuts. But these wretched Papoos were, I knew, often starving, although those that Paul and I lived amongst near the Abrolhos were not cannibals.

Suddenly Zolca started and drew my attention to a dried and shrivelled head, lying a short distance away. It was the head of a Mongol. One, perhaps two, of the pirates had escaped and made their way overland to this bay, where they had remained watching for another junk to come along, and meanwhile living on the fish with which the bay swarmed. Here, then, they had lingered until surprised and slaughtered by the Papoos.

"This is a bay of evil omen," said Zolca; "let us go home."

We were soon skirting the mangroves once more and speedily reached our own bay early the next morning.

The wet season was now approaching and by the following autumn, which in Terra Australis is exactly opposite to ours, being in April and May, we anticipated having our crops, of one sort or another, in good order again.

Zolca was growing more resigned to his lot, and Azolta recovered some of her wonted spirits, so that life promised to flow on in the same even tide as before.

CHAPTER XVII.

The great Catastrophe—Extinction of the
Quadrucos—The Death of Zolca and of Azolta—I am left
alone.

IT was the month of March when the great catastrophe occurred. The wet season had not been a particularly heavy one, and no sign was given us of the impending calamity.

One morning the sun rose red in a haze which reminded me much of the morning Hoogstraaten and I watched the *Selwaert* dashed helplessly on to the bar of Wreck Bay. The wind from the north-west began to moan dismally about noon-tide. Then the rain-clouds commenced to scud across the sky, and as darkness fell the rain commenced. This was nothing, snug and secure in our well-built houses we heeded not the growing storm, and slept soundly through all its increasing fury. In the morning we found that a great gale was blowing, the river was running strong, and the sea was raging on the outside coast.

All day the turmoil increased, and towards dusk the bay itself began to feel the influence of the wind, and the rollers from the ocean swept in, and broke in surf upon the beach, smashing our boats, and hurling them on the sand.[B]

That night no one slept much, the river was overflowing its banks, and flooding our plantations, and, sheltered though we were in the valley, the tempestuous blasts that swept up from seaward, seemed to make the very earth tremble. Never before did man witness such a war of the elements.

Foot by foot, the river began to rise with great rapidity. The rain never ceased, but fell in continuous sheets. Now and again, a vivid flash of lightning, followed almost instantaneously by a deafening peal of thunder, illuminated the valley, and afforded a view of the terrifying scene. Still the river encroached on the level ground, and began to invade the houses.

Suddenly, a sound broke on my ear, coming from seaward, a roar, such as I had never heard before—a roar that seemed to unite in its voice, sea, storm, and flood! Some instinct told me what it was, and calling to the others, I shouted to them to make for the ridge. Azolta had one child, I had the other and had also to help poor, crippled Zolca. His wife followed us, and in the darkness, we plunged into the muddy flood, and made for the ridge.

I called to the rest of the Quadrucos, but they were watching the upper part of the river, and did not heed the great roar rushing up from the sea. Closer it came, and the water suddenly leapt up about us, and we had to swim amidst eddies and whirlpools. We were torn apart, and the child escaped from my grasp.

When I regained the surface I was swept against someone who was battling helplessly against the furious tide, and felt that it was Zolca. A flash of lightning showed me the ridge, close to us, and with my assistance Zolca reached it, and sank exhausted on the muddy slope, although the water still surged and swept around us.

Suddenly, I heard a cry! Yes! even through that din and confusion I heard it, although now it seems scarcely believable.

"Deedreek! Deedreek! Save me!"

I left Zolca, and splashed through the water in the direction I had heard the cry. Another kindly flash and glare, and cannonade of thunder, showed me Azolta clinging to the stem of a tree. I plunged in, and brought her to the land, and then literally felt my way back to where I had left Zolca, and found him. He managed to get up and scramble to higher ground, and in a short time, we three, the sole survivors of the overwhelming calamity that had befallen us, met together.

As yet, in the darkness, we did not know the worst, but we knew, at least, that the worst had befallen ourselves. Our children and Zolca's wife must have perished, and of the Quadruco people I dared not think. A gleam of lightning showed me an overhanging rock which I knew, and under its shelter I managed to get my two companions saved somewhat from the pitiless rain and wind.

Zolca and Azolta sank down exhausted, and I could only sit with my back against the rock and think. I knew what had happened. The long-continued gale had backed the tide up in the gorge I have before mentioned as terminating the end of the valley. This blocked the outflow of the flood-waters of the river, and they, of course, commenced to overflow the valley. Then, hurried on by the fierce blast from the north-west, an immense tidal wave had swept into the bay, rushed up the gorge, beating back the flood-waters, hurling them on to the doomed valley, and burying everything under fathoms of salt water and mud-laden flood.

The fitful gleams of vivid lightning showed me the surface of a storm-swept sea where once was our valley.

In abject misery the weary night passed over, and when the lagging dawn at last asserted itself, I could see nothing but an estuary of tossing, yellow water, still pelted by the terrible rain-fall.

Zolca was still alive, and when the light was strong he looked imploringly at me. I raised him in my arms, and he saw the water on the slopes of the valley, covering everything belonging to him and his people. He gave one cry when he realized all the disaster, and, sinking back in my arms, his great heart broken, died without a shudder.

Roused by the death-wail of her twin-brother, Azolta rose from her sleep of exhaustion. One glance at Zolca's face and glazed eyes showed her the truth. She threw herself on his body, and begged and prayed him to return to her. I tried to loosen her arms from the corpse, but could not do so without using force, and I had to stay there and listen to her moans without being able to help her.

The gale had blown itself out by mid-day, and the rain ceased for a while.

Azolta feebly called to me, and when I stooped over her I saw that I should soon be truly alone. She put her arms around my neck, and as I pressed my lips to hers, her soul went out to join Zolca's in the great Silent Country.

How long I remained stupefied with grief I know not. I was roused by the noise of rushing water, and saw that the flood was now falling rapidly. I looked languidly on; I felt no interest in it. I only wanted to die, and be with my people again. I was weak and exhausted, without enough energy to take my own life; so I sat on in stupid semi-consciousness through the gloomy evening and the gloomier night, until at last the morning broke, bright, sunny, and beautiful—a morning that mocked the desolation it revealed.

Strange to say, Zolca had still the old cutlass in his belt, and taking this I went a little way up the ridge, and commenced the weary task of digging two graves. I need not recount my labour. I dug them side by side, east and west, and when I had placed my dear ones in their last home, I covered them in, and heaped stones above them, forming two mounds. Some of the rocks I carried from a distance, as there were none sufficiently large in the neighbourhood to secure my dead from being disturbed by the Papoos.

When I had finished my grievous labour I went to look at the valley. The river had returned to the confinement of its banks, but the whole of the town had as completely disappeared as if it had never existed. The mud houses, soaked through by being under water so long, had melted away with the backward rush of the flood, and the mighty torrent had carried everything out to sea, save what it had left buried under two feet of mud. Mud covered everything in the valley, and I did not descend into it.

I was faint from hunger, and remembered that at the cannon mounted on the elevation commanding the bay, and at the one on the headland, provisions had been safely stored in case of a surprise. There I turned my steps, and found that the one on the elevation had escaped the fury of the flood, but the great wave had swept over the headland and destroyed our little battery. It mattered not—there was nothing now to defend.

I found an ample supply of provisions of one sort or another—smoked fish, and cocoa-nuts, and other things,—and some of these I conveyed to the overhanging rock where my wife and brother died.

I determined to rest here for a while, until I had recovered from the shock. I used to visit the graves daily, and occupy myself with adding stones to the mounds, and making them square and level.

The idea of suicide had deserted me, and a kind of apathy had set in. Perhaps Hoogstraaten might revisit the coast, and take me away.

I never went into the valley, even when the sun had hardened the mud. I got the little food I wanted from the store at the cannon, and my companions were the two graves, where I used to sit and talk to the dead for many hours during the day.

One day, when sitting thus, it suddenly occurred to me that I was the only European in this great mysterious land of the south, of which even such a bold and experienced navigator as Hoogstraaten knew not the limits. With the thought a great horror of loneliness came upon me, and I shrieked aloud, calling on God to kill me at once and end my sufferings. Then I knelt by Azolta's grave, and whispered to her to come out and keep me company in this awful solitude; and then—I knew no more!

[B] The hurricanes that break on the north-west coast of
Australia equal in fury the typhoons of the northern tropic.
Vessels belonging to the pearling fleet have been carried far
into the mangroves and left high and dry. They are locally
known as "willy-willys".

CHAPTER XVIII.

My Reason is Restored—Rescue by Dutch Ships—The return to Holland—I settle down there.

OF the great blank that came into my life I can recall but little. I have dim memories of the strange fancies I had during that time, but how long it lasted I cannot say, or at least I had no clue when at last reason reasserted itself. I have cause to believe since that it must have been nearly two years. I do not think I was unhappy during that time, and I suppose I had more than my natural strength and skill for hunting. Often Azolta and Zolca, and sometimes Paul, were with me in my distorted imaginings, but these ghosts never came at the same time; even a madman could not imagine that.

When my senses returned—and they came back suddenly—my first discovery was that I was lying on the sand of a strange shore. I looked around, but all was new to me. I remembered everything of the flood that had happened, but it seemed only yesterday that it had occurred. How then did I come where I was?

I rose and began to pace the beach. I was naked, but beside me, where I had been lying, was the old cutlass covered with rust. The tide was low, and had left many large pools in the rocks; looking into one of these I started with dismay, for I thought I was the victim of magic.

My hair, long and matted, hung down my back; my beard had grown far down my breast, and both hair and beard were white as the foam of the sea! I was burnt a deep brown by the sun, and my eyes seemed to look back at me from the glassy water with an unnatural brightness. This is what Nature's mirror showed me, and I could scarcely credit my senses.

I walked up and down, and exhausted myself in speculations regarding this wondrous transformation, but could only at last come to the conclusion that I had been wandering about in a demented condition for some time. But for how long? And above all where was I?

It was early in the morning, and the sun was on my right

hand as I looked seaward. I was, then, on the northern coast of Terra Australis, and must have made my way up with some mad idea of reaching Java.

I found a pile of shell-fish I had collected, and a smouldering fire; so that I must have been amongst the Papoos and got fire from them, and carried a burning stick with me always, after their fashion.

I roasted the shell-fish on the coals and ate them with satisfaction, for I was hungry. Searching about I came on a spring of fresh water, emerging from the bank where it met the beach. Of this I drank heartily, and then, climbing the bank, looked around at the new country where I found myself. An open plain, with many of the tall, white mounds on it made by the ants, ran back for some distance, and beyond, many miles away, rose a lofty tier of mountain ranges higher than any I had yet seen in Terra Australis. These lay to the south; had I crossed that great barrier during my madness? I know now that I must have done so.

There was no smoke to be seen anywhere, no sign of life, and I returned to the beach and sat down to try and think out the past. But, beyond the point I have recounted, my memory failed me, and I found that it only fatigued me to try and piece my scattered fancies together.

I desisted, and went along the shore to gather food. I was fortunate enough to find a large fish, stranded by the tide, in a hole in a flat rock, and in addition easily obtained a large quantity of shell-fish.

I returned to my lair where the fire was smouldering, gathered wood to keep it burning all through the night, and when darkness fell, lay down to sleep on the sand. All fear or dread of loneliness had departed, I felt almost contented as I lay and watched the beautiful southern constellations, until sleep gradually stole over me, and I slumbered dreamlessly until morning. The air was soft and balmy, and the sun just rising when I awoke. There was a little ripple on the water and I stood gazing out on the peaceful scene, and drinking in the fresh morning air. I felt strong and well, refreshed by my night's sleep, and turned to go and hunt for my breakfast.

But what was that! I gasped with astonishment and then—shouted for joy!

Three large ships, standing close inshore, were coming up slowly from the eastward. I ran to my fire and piled all the wood on I had, then gathered green boughs, bushes, and anything that would make a good smoke. I worked hard at this until I had a dense column of smoke ascending in the now calm air; for the light breeze had fallen on the land, although out at sea the ships seemed to still carry it, for they were nearly abreast of me before it dropped altogether, and they furled their sails and anchored.

I felt confident they would send ashore for water, even if my smoke did not attract them, which they might put down to the Papoos. I was right; two or three boats were soon coming towards the land.

As the foremost one neared the shore I went to meet it. The men lay on their oars, and stared at me with fear and amazement; and no wonder, for I must have presented a strange figure indeed, with bronzed body, flowing white hair and beard, and in my hand the rusty cutlass.

I shouted to them in Dutch, and the officer immediately ordered the men to pull in.

"Who are you?" he demanded.

"I am Diedrich Buys," I returned, "and have been living in another part of this country for many years."

"Diedrich Buys! Why, we have orders, I believe, to call at your settlement and see if you require anything."

"My settlement exists no longer," I replied sadly, and shortly told the officer of the calamitous flood that had overwhelmed us.

"You must come on board to De Witt at once," he said. "Is there any water about here?"

I pointed out the place and, after directing the men to it, we were rowed back to the ship, the officer handing me a large cloak to cover myself with.

Once on deck the officer led me to a dignified looking man, who with the others was staring at me in some amazement.

"Captain De Witt," he said, "this is Herr Diedrich Buys, whom I have been fortunate enough to rescue from these barren shores."

De Witt stepped forward, and shook me warmly by the hand.

"I see," he said, "that some terrible misfortune must have happened; but before you say anything, you must first be clothed and refreshed."

At a word from him the officer conducted me to a large, roomy cabin, under the high poop. Here a sailor brought in a tub, which he filled with salt water, and the officer, who had gone away, returned with a suit of clothes, shoes, and linen. I enjoyed the bath, and found that the clothes fitted me to perfection. When nearly dressed, the captain's servant came to the door, bringing with him comb and scissors. He cut my luxuriant locks off, and reduced my beard to the short, pointed peak now worn.

When I emerged from the cabin, and saw myself in a large mirror there was in the main cabin, I could scarce believe in the transformation.

Refreshment had been provided, and after partaking of some the officer who had brought me on board came down to conduct me on deck. I saw him give a start at my appearance, then he laughed cordially.

"Truly, Herr Buys, you look more like the man described by Captain Hoogstraaten than you did some short time back."

I smiled in return, and we went on deck.

Here we found the captains and some of the officers of the other two ships, who had been signalled to come on board. Grave, dignified men they all were, as befitted the scientific navigators of a great maritime nation.

De Witt presented me to them, and I told my tale. There were many expressions of sorrow and sympathy at the extinction of such an interesting race.

The chart compiled by Hoogstraaten was then produced, and our situation found. The valley of the Quadrucos was marked on it, and we found that, if I had come in a straight line, I must have come over three hundred miles, whereas I probably wandered about and made it three or four times as much.

On inquiry, I learned that Hoogstraaten had left the Company's service, and now lived on his estate in Holland.

The ships being watered, and a fair wind having sprung up, we made sail, and in time came to Wreck Bay. Here we landed, and found that it had suffered like the other bay, and that every vestige of the old encampment had been obliterated. Making sail once more we finally reached the bay of the Quadrucos, and I piloted the ships in.

De Witt and the others landed to visit the valley, but I could not bear to go. Instead, I made a journey to the graves of my lost ones; I found them untouched, and knelt down and shed some bitter tears over them.

The party which had gone to the valley did not return until late, as I had told them of the upper portion, where probably the cocoa-nut trees had not been destroyed. This proved to be the case, and we were able to obtain a good supply from there for all the ships.

De Witt told me that, but for knowing the truth, he could not have believed that the town had ever existed. Luxuriant grass, up to a man's waist, now grew all over the site. The only relics they had found were two or three of the roughly-made Quadruco swords. We visited the batteries, and De Witt had the two brass cannons conveyed on board his vessel.

"These are your private property, Herr Buys," he said, "and it is no good leaving them here for the Mongols; the Company will pay you good rix-dollars for them when we reach Batavia."

Next morning early we sailed, and I said farewell for ever to the bay where I had undergone so many vicissitudes, and to the desolate land of Terra Australis or New Holland, as I now heard it was called.

As De Witt's discovery-voyage had been on the north coast of the great continent, and he had only been instructed to call at the Quadruco Bay to see how we were progressing, his work was over, and we shaped a straight course to Batavia.

I was cordially welcomed by the Governor, who obtained for me a passage in a homeward-bound ship, and furnished me with letters to influential people in Holland. Having bade good-bye to my many kind friends, I sailed for home.

The voyage was uneventful; and after some months I found myself once more in my native Harlem.

I put up at a tavern and made inquiries as to my family. Alas! I found that a sickness, which had visited the town some years back, had carried off my father, mother, and elder brother—in fact, they had died soon after Hoogstraaten's visit. My father's estate, which was somewhat considerable, had descended, in my absence, to my young brother, who was but a child when I left home in the ill-fated *Batavia*. I turned my steps towards my home and asked for my brother.

I was shown into his private office. I found him a young man with a somewhat hard face, who gazed curiously at me and asked my business.

"I am your brother Diedrich," I replied, "just returned from Batavia."

He sprang up from his chair, to welcome me, as I foolishly thought, but it was quite otherwise.

"I know no brother Diedrich!" he cried. "There was one of our family of that name, but he is an outlaw, and dare not show his face in Holland. You are some impostor who has heard of him, and come here to claim my property."

111

"I never thought of your property," I returned hotly. "I am no impostor, and no outlaw; I have long since been pardoned for a crime I never committed."

"I will not listen to you," he said nervously; "I do not believe you. When we last heard of my brother he was living with a tribe of savage Indians in some wild country, and he is there still. Leave this house, or the servants shall thrust you out."

I stepped up to him in red-hot rage.

"Since this is my reception I will assert my rights. I will leave my house now, and when I return it will be you who will have to leave. Look here!" I went on, drawing from my pocket the letters I had from the governor of Java, which I had not yet delivered; "does an impostor usually carry such credentials as these?" and I showed him the superscriptions, and the great seal of the Company on the back.

He blenched visibly, and muttered something about "forgeries". I gave him a look of contempt, and left the house.

I was cut to the heart. From savages, from strangers, from everyone, even pirates, I had received gentle, kindly treatment, and now my own brother, my sole relation, cast me out as an impostor seeking to rob him.

A handsome, richly-dressed man came by and gazed curiously at me, as many people did on account of my dark face and white hair and beard. He turned, followed, and spoke to me.

"What ails it, friend?" he asked, in a cordial voice. "You look like a stranger, and one who has travelled far and suffered much, and in such men I am always interested."

I looked at him, but there was nothing in his face but the most manly sympathy.

"True! I have travelled farther than most men, and suffered more," I replied; "but never so much as I have during the last half-hour."

He gazed earnestly at me, and then at the house I had just left.

"That is the house of the merchant Buys," he said, "and you—surely it cannot be that you are Diedrich, of whom my dear friend, Captain Hoogstraaten, has so often told me."

"I am Diedrich Buys," I replied.

He held out both hands and shook mine warmly.

"I am Count Van de Burg," he said, "and you must at once return home with me, and tell me your tale at leisure."

I accompanied him to his mansion, and on the way asked after Hoogstraaten.

"He lives on his estate outside of Amsterdam," he returned, "where we will soon visit him, and also see the great chart of his voyages laid down in the Groote Zaal in the Stadhuys of that city."

The count, I found afterwards, was an enthusiatic patron of oversea-discovery. He was the soul of generosity, and no broken-down sailor or penniless adventurer ever appealed to him for assistance in vain.

I have little more to add. Hoogstraaten heard my account of the disaster with the most profound grief and sorrow.

My brother, when he found what friends I had, surrendered at discretion; but I merely took enough of my father's property to supply my simple wants.

I live near Hoogstraaten's estate, and he and Count Van de Burg are the only friends I have, or want; for my heart is far away in two graves in the lonely land of Terra Australis.

APPENDIX.

DE GONNEVILLE left Honfleur in the month of June of the year 1503, in the good ship *L'Espoir*; and after having rounded the Cape of Good Hope he was assailed by tempestuous weather and driven into calmer latitudes. A tedious spell of calms forced him, for want of water, to make for the first land he could sight. The flight of some birds coming from the south decided him to run a course to the southward, and after a few days' sail he landed on the coast of a large territory, at the mouth of a fine river which he compared to the river Orne at Caen. There he remained six months, repairing his vessel, holding meanwhile amicable relations with the natives. He left the great Austral land, to which he gave the name of "Southern Indies", on the 3rd July, 1504, taking with him two of the natives, one of these being the son of the chief of the tribe amongst whom he had resided. On the return voyage no land was seen until the day after the Feast of St. Denis, on the 10th of October of the same year; but, on nearing the coast of France the ship was attacked, off the islands of Guernsey and Jersey, by an English privateer, who robbed the navigators of all they had brought with them from the land they had visited: the most important loss being the journal of the expedition. On their arrival at Honfleur De Gonneville immediately entered a plaint before the Admiralty Court of Normandy, and wrote a report of his voyage which was signed by the principal officers of the vessel.

The following is a translation of the title of this document:—

"*Judicial declaration made before the Admiralty Court of Normandy by Sieur de Gonneville, at the request of the King's Procurator, respecting the voyage of the good ship 'L'Espoir', of the port of Honfleur, to the Southern Indies.*"

The account of the erection of the great Cross runs thus:—

"Intending to leave some memorial that this country had been visited by Christians, they erected a large wooden cross, thirty-five feet high, and painted over, placed on an eminence in view of the sea. This they did with much ceremony on the day of Pentecost, 1504; the Cross being carried by the captain and his officers, all barefooted, accompanied by the King Arosca and the principal Indians. After them followed the crew under arms, and singing the Litany. They were accompanied by a crowd of Indians, to whom they gave to understand the meaning of the ceremony as well as they could. Having set up the Cross, they fired volleys of their cannon and small arms, charging the Indians to keep carefully and honour the monument they had set up.

"Having refitted the ship, and being willing, after the manner of those who discover strange countries, to bring some of the natives back with them, they persuaded the King Arosca to let them have one of his sons, promising the father that they would bring him back in twenty moons, with others who should teach them the use of firearms, and how to make mirrors, axes, knives, and other things they used amongst Christians."

.   .   .   .

Being unable to keep his word as to the return of Prince Essomeric, the tradition goes that De Gonneville settled some of his property on him, gave him his name, and married him to a relative, as some compensation. What the relative thought of it does not appear. The grandson of Essomeric by this marriage is said to have been a priest, and, under the name of J. B. Paulmier, was canon of the Cathedral Church of St. Pierre de Lizieux.

The fact of the carven stone head is thus told by Sir George Grey, who discovered it in the north-west, about that part of the coast where De Gonneville was supposed to have landed:—

"I was moving on when we observed the profile of a human face and head cut out in a sandstone rock which fronted the cave. This rock was so hard that to have removed such a large portion of it with no better tools than a knife and hatchet made of stone, such as the Australian natives generally possess, would have been a work of great labour. The whole of the work was good, and far superior to what a savage race could be supposed capable of executing. The only proof of antiquity that it bore about it was that all the edges of the cutting were rounded, and perfectly smooth—much more so than they could have been from any other cause than long exposure to atmospheric influences."

The two graves in which I have buried Zolca and Azolta were also discovered by Sir George Grey, and thus described by him:—

"*April 6.* We halted a few hundred yards from two remarkable heaps of stones of the same kind as those I have before mentioned.

"*April 7.* This morning I started off before dawn, and opened the most southern of the two mounds of stone, which presented the following curious facts. 1st. They were both placed due east and west with great regularity. 2nd. They were both exactly of the same length, but different in breadth and height. 3rd. They were not formed altogether of small stones from the place on which they stood, but many were portions of very distant rocks, which must have been brought by human hands. My own opinion concerning these heaps of stones had been that they were tombs: and this opinion remains unaltered, though we found no bones in the mound, only a great deal of fine mould, having a damp, dank smell. The antiquity of the one we opened appeared to be very great—I should say two or three hundred years."

Whether these strange discoveries of Grey's, including the well-known cave paintings, point to the existence once of a colony of semi-civilized people cannot well be determined. The non-existence of ruins of any sort can easily be accounted for by the fact that they built their houses of mud which, after being abandoned to the mercy of successive tropical wet seasons, would soon disappear. The work found differs so entirely from the ordinary rude memorials of the aborigines that there is room for speculation on the subject.